Cinnomon,
Enjoy the story!
Cori Wawrley

The Treasures We Seek

A Novel

Cori Wamsley

Aurora Corialis Publishing

Pittsburgh, PA

Paperback ISBN: 978-1-958481-15-8

Ebook ISBN: 978-1-958481-16-5

Printed in the United States of America

Cover by Karen Captline, BetterBe Creative

Edited by Allison Hrip, Aurora Corialis Publishing

Other Books by Cori Wamsley

Braving the Shore (women's fiction)

Twenty Won: 21 Female Entrepreneurs Share their
Stories of Resilience During a Global Pandemic
(anthology)

Living Kindly: Bold Conversations about the Power of
Kindness (anthology)

Monkey Mermaid Magic (children's)

The SPARK Method: How to Write a Book for Your
Business Fast (nonfiction)

The Knight and the Ninjas (children's)

Confessions of the Editor Brigand (women's fiction)

Martina Mackenzie: The Isle of Bala Zopyre (middle
grade)

Martina Mackenzie: The Palace of Glass (middle grade)

Martina Mackenzie: The Enchanted Carousel (middle
grade)

Martina Mackenzie: The Diana's Eye (middle grade)

Praise for *The Treasures We Seek*

"Cori Wamsley's novel effortlessly transports readers to a time of genuine self-discovery, when we experience revelations about life as we are living it. With a vibrant and energetic tone, Wamsley imparts the thrill of introspection, gracefully sharing life's insights without prescription. The narrative beautifully weaves history, culture, and architecture together with a thread of serendipity, into a rich Italian tapestry that mirrors the multi-dimensional experience of individual exploration and adventure. Wamsley's blend of wisdom and wit creates an engaging, educational, and enchanting treasure well worth digging into."

~ Amy Hooper Hanna, CEO of AhHA! Coaching & Consulting, and Co-author of *For She Who Grieves: Practical Wisdom for Living Hope*

———

"When Kenzi decides to take a whirlwind trip to Italy—to work at an archeological site—she has no way of knowing that she'll dig up far more than just priceless artifacts. She'll also unearth a more authentic version of herself. *The Treasures We Seek* is a warm, thoughtful, and powerfully quiet story of self-actualization. Readers who struggle with prioritizing their own needs instead of everyone else's will find much to love in this book. So will readers who appreciate breaking out of routines and trying things that are wholly and thrillingly new. *The Treasures We Seek* shows how letting our insecurities crumble like shards of pottery can be the first step in seeing everything finally come together."

~Stacey Elza, Author of *Falling Lessons*

———

"She's done it again! Cori Wamsley's *The Treasures We Seek* is a gift! The friendship between Kenzi and Lauren is a story that most people wouldn't understand – unless they've been through a trauma and found their biggest supporter in the most unlikely person. Their friendship gives hope to women who think their "BFF Soulmate" doesn't exist. Cori also does a fantastic job of telling the stories of Kenzi and her family, including some familiar to nearly everyone mother / daughter dynamics between Kenzi and her mom.

"The biggest chunk of the book is spent following Kenzi and Lauren in Italy, digging for artifacts. There were moments I swear I could smell the lemon trees and taste the cuisine right along with the teams of people who were on the adventure. The research Cori did was intense; I learned so much about Italy, a "bucket list" trip for me as my maternal great grandparents came to the U.S. from Italy.

"This was a fantastic read, appropriate for women of all ages. When I closed the book, I wanted to get pasta and wine with my best friends and tell them how much I love and appreciate them!"

~ Kelli Komondor, Visibility Strategist, Speaker, Author of *Twenty Won*

———

"*The Treasures We Seek* is an engaging story about tangible and intangible treasures in life. It's a terrific read for those with wanderlust, as the Italian countryside vividly comes to life and is the perfect setting for an archeological treasure hunt. Cori Walmsley has done her research and beautifully describes the Italian experience, providing the perfect read for those who dream of stepping outside their comfort zone on a journey of self-discovery."

~ Kim Adley, Author and Owner of Passport to Pittsburgh, a Custom Tour Company

———

"I read *The Treasures We Seek* in an afternoon; it was so delightful and heartening of a story! So many pieces of Kenzie's interiority truly resonated with me as an 'awkward' adult who was late diagnosed with ADHD and ASD. And I have a friend who has celiac, too. Kenzi's issues around social interactions and foods, all are so very authentic.

"This coming of age story was so good, and such a great reminder of how we all continue to learn to human better by letting go of the restrictive puppet strings of our upbringing and past negative experiences. Of how we can learn to do better and help others by sharing our own stories. This book is an afternoon delight that will leave you with hope and a smile."

~ Heather Romero, The Happy Typist

Praise for *Braving the Shore*

"Cori Wamsley writes an intriguing story, one she has artfully woven with the unbreakable bonds of sisterly love and the infinite connection to the spiritual realm."

~ J.D. Wylde, Author of *When Trouble Comes Calling* and *When Push Comes to Shove*

———

"Chelsea's journey of perseverance at all costs was inspiring. As a mom to two young girls, seeing the strength of her relationship with Jocelyn struck a personal chord. *Braving the Shore* demonstrates how overcoming great challenges and discovering your life's path is all the more meaningful when it's done alongside those you love."

~ Kimber Wood, @now__reading__kw book blog on Instagram

———

"This tale of sisterhood, love, and how the Universe works in mysterious ways is one that won't soon be forgotten! The book was satisfying from start to finish—it brought all my senses to life; I could feel the ocean, smell and taste the goodies in the bakery, and see and hear the characters as if they were old, familiar friends. These real, relatable women could be any of us if the circumstances were just right. *Braving the Shore* is an incredible read."

~ Kelli A. Komondor, Bestselling Author of *Twenty Won: 21 Female Entrepreneurs Share Their Stories of Business Resilience During a Global Crisis,* Speaker, Entrepreneur

----

"*Braving the Shore* is a delightful story that shows us how important it is to listen, remember who we are, and make brave choices. It will be a great book for anyone needing a sweet, little nudge to be courageous, receive support, and claim who they are."

~ Gabrielle Smith Noye

"Cori Wamsley sparks intrigue in her newest novel *Braving the Shore* by bringing reality and the ethereal together to find balance in the chaos for the lives of identical twin sisters, Chelsea and Jocelyn. When the two sisters reunite, a traumatic event creates what feels like a rift in the amazing universe that they have known all their lives.

"Chelsea heard, 'Sometimes the Universe has to shake things up to get you to correct your course.' Through meditation, movement on promptings from the spirit world, remembering sweet family memories, baking Grandmother's special pastry recipes, and the insatiable urge to sink toes in the sandy shore . . . Chelsea discovers the answers to so many perplexing life questions that she had just encountered for the first time.

"Cori Wamsley is a brilliant and colorfully descriptive author whose writing of *Braving the Shore* draws in the audience, allowing the reader to feel like they are in the midst of the storyline. One may be able to experience the aroma coming from the bakery kitchen, feel the sandy shore as a peaceful refuge, see the colors of the sea glass and understand its symbolism of healing in the story, feel when someone's glance makes the heart flutter with glee, to name a few.

"Additionally, Cori is a gifted book writing coach, author, and editor who helps other authors find their authenticity and authority in their own stories to share with the world. Her book *The SPARK*

Method is a great tool for those looking to write a book. It is a privilege to know Cori, read her stories, and be instructed by her with my own writing."

~Sue E. Fattibene, Life Coach, Author of *The Day the Angel Sat Beside Me*, Inspirational Speaker

Table of Contents

Chapter 1

"That's the third one this month ..." I gaze into the mirror at yet another gray hair. I'm getting ready for work and spot it shimmering rebelliously in the sea of my dark brown tresses, sprouting right from the part, looking like a piece of tinsel on a bitter dark chocolate bar.

Festive.

Scientifically speaking, I know I can't blame the gray hair on stress. I know it's genetic. And I also know that I'm blessed in that department. Neither of my parents had much gray till their 50s, so I know I have time.

But that doesn't make me feel any less urgent to get my act together. I started to a few months ago, but you know ...

Nothing like a good shake up in "the plans"—life plans, all the stuff that you're supposed to do, including a house, family, 6-figure job, burnout, etc.—to make you feel a little on edge. God, I just turned 30. Sometimes I feel like my clock is tick tick ticking ... and I still haven't gotten my life figured out.

I know what you're thinking. It's not like I live in my mom's basement. I let out a huge sigh as the internal battle wages on. I own a duplex. And I have a job that I love.

And no, *a job* doesn't make you a grownup. And it doesn't mean that you're fulfilled and satisfied. It literally means that you're employed.

Again, I know I'm lucky in that department. I smile, recalling how much I love what I do. I breathe it. I sweat it. I live it.

And that's kind of the problem ...

I wouldn't say that I'm a workaholic, *per se*, but given the options, an hour of overtime is waaaay more appealing than happy hour.

And so is a good book. Or movie. I'm not terribly picky about how I spend my alone time.

But we're *supposed* to do what makes us happy, right? And if happiness to me is sketching a new home or spending an entire Saturday with my nose in a book or grabbing a glass of wine and chatting with Macy and Lauren, then why worry?

I keep asking myself that. *Why worry? Am I worried?* Maybe. *A tad? A skosh?* I know by this point I was supposed to have fallen head over heels for someone, my hand weighed down with an obligatory giant diamond, and have 2.5 kids and a minivan <shudder>, but is that for me?

What about my purpose? What *is* a purpose? And why can't someone just email me with it?

I decided after my disastrous last relationship … which ended about a year ago, a story for another time … that the head over heels thing sounds incredibly painful, debilitating, life-threatening even. Who wants a concussion? And wasn't there an author who said that she would never fall in love because the men in her books, the ones she creates, are way better than real men anyway? That no living man could ever stand up to the man on the page? Something like that.

So, what's the point?

I haven't sworn off men. I look. I admire. I just don't feel that uterus-pulsing desire to grab a "good one" and pop out babies. (My brother has four, which is technically enough for both of us.) I did feel that once. But honestly, I prefer my job: chatting with a couple about their perfect home and then making it happen for them is so much more satisfying than chatting with a stranger about his perfect future and deciding that I'm too much my own woman to just cave and draw it for him. Being an architect is about making dreams come true. It's about being a people pleaser, and I'm cool with that. That's easy.

Being a girlfriend is not.

Sorry, not sorry.

Relationships don't work when one person is a people pleaser and the other is, well, taking advantage. I've done that before.

God, I need a lot of concealer today. Serious dark circles. What the hell? I didn't even think the weekend was that rough.

I did Thanksgiving with Lauren's family across town this year, and Macy came with, since her parents are visiting family in Kenya right now and her siblings are scattered all over the US.

Lauren's family was so welcoming to us Thanksgiving orphans. And Mom and Stan will be back in Pittsburgh for Christmas, so it wasn't a huge deal that I didn't see them.

But here's the snag. Mom wants to do Christmas *at my house*. My tiny half of the duplex. Maybe it's not so tiny. But it's still a lot of people to host. Mom, Stan, Grandma Claudia, Declan and Sarah, and their four kids . . . And me, of course. She called last night to ask me. I mean *tell* me. But she made it sound like she was asking.

I'm sure I can do it. I'm just nervous because I've never done it before. Since my brother Declan got married, it's just been easier to do it at his house ... with all the kids. Sarah said it's really hard to get all their stuff together and drag them around. But they are all out of diapers now, so that's less stuff. In fact, the kids became so portable this year that Declan and Sarah took them all to Paris for the fall to live in a cute little apartment and learn French and eat pastries, and wow, the pictures are gorgeous.

He's a business coach, so he has that kind of flexibility. And Sarah manages a social media management company. Makes it all easy. They just put team members in place to help out with the biz and hired a sweet older French lady, Marguerite, to home school the littles and handle some of the cooking and cleaning, *s'il vous plait*.

Anyway, Declan is living the dream, but their Pittsburgh house is rented out till the 22nd, so they aren't leaving Europe till the 23rd. Who knows if they will get over the jetlag, let alone put up Christmas decorations in time! Mom wants things to be perfect. I get it. I can host Christmas. No sweat, right?

It's just an extra *nine* people to cook for ... and over half of them are used to having French cuisine prepared for them every day. *Welcome! Grilled cheese, anyone?* Bon appétit!

Where's my lipstick? In my purse. Right. I threw it in last night.

Now where did I set my purse? Probably in my bedroom.

My bed is neatly made up with my new winter comforter. It's white. Like snow. And I've tossed a gray furry throw jauntily across the bottom corner of the bed. I love the way it drapes. A single red pillow with the word "Joy" embroidered across it graces the pair of sleeping pillows at the head of the bed. Simple and perfect.

The purse, however, is not on my bed. It's on the dresser. In fact, it's the only thing on the dresser besides the book I was reading last night, *A Holiday in the City*, which is such a great romance. Love!

I snag the lipstick from my purse and apply it quickly. Then, I grab my purse and work bag and dash to the garage.

I slip on black loafers that are waiting for me by the garage door. They look great with my outfit, which is simple and professional: black sweater, black and white houndstooth pants ... I swear I own things in other colors ... red gemstone statement necklace.

I throw on my coat, which, yes, is black, and hop in my car. Fine, the car is gray. Man, I like neutrals.

It's easy to splash things up with a bright colored bag or pillow or vase or whatever and have a clean look.

The first day back at the office after Thanksgiving break is bound to be busy, but it's always a good busy. The kind of busy where you take a deep breath of your coffee, sip it slowly, and dive into your inbox in the quiet of your office.

Maybe it's weird, but I love it.

I put the car in reverse, leave the garage, and head for that quiet.

Baker & Willow is honestly a great place to work. It's the first architectural firm that took an interest in my design work and gave me a serious position designing homes instead of asking if I wanted to assist the head designers, like the bigger firms. Plus, I love that it's just outside of Pittsburgh. It's easy to get to, and I didn't have to move somewhere where I didn't know anyone to get started on my career ... seven years ago.

I've been pretty comfortable here.

Even easier: it's only a15-minute drive from my development. Baker & Willow was contracted for design work in Chestnut Acres, so I had first bid on the duplex. Easy peasy.

Maybe too easy ...

But hey, it's all good right now, till I'm ready to shake things up and spread my wings.

I guide my car onto the highway and head south to the next exit. Traffic isn't terrible heading south, away from the city. The other way, no thank you! It's thick and about to get even worse. Rush hour is no joke around here.

I turn into the business park where Baker & Willow's offices are and park in the first row, close to the building. I love being an early bird ...for several reasons.

Not only do I get ah-mazing parking, but I also get to avoid a lot of the small talk with people wandering into the building to start their day.

Thanks, but no thanks. I'm happy with the quiet and not discussing the weather with that odd older guy in accounting who talks to EVERYONE about nothing.

"Good morning, Rachel!" I chirp to our receptionist. She is the sweetest lady.

Rachel smiles. "Coffee is brewing, Kenzi." She points at my empty hand. "Make sure you grab it before the rest of them get here."

"No worries with that. You're the best."

I unlock my office and slip inside. Ah, normalcy. Quiet. I drop off my stuff, slip back to the coffee station with my "PERFCT" mug—one of my birthday presents from Lauren, she's funny—and return to my desk with caffeine. Time to dive into the email.

As I peruse my inbox, a few souls straggle into the building. Half an hour later, most of my coworkers show up. It's a small company, so there aren't a ton of people anyway, but we share a parking lot with all the other businesses in the building, sooooo ... best to be early.

I don't really look up, but I notice the stream of people passing my door. A couple people tap on the glass and wave, so I wave back. It's a nice group here, and I talk with a few of them, but I'm not really close with anyone.

Around 9, I'm catching up on my to-do list, having finished my emails from break, when I hear a tap on my door. I glance up and see Logan Oliver, the head of sales and marketing, smiling and waving. He has an adorable, crooked smile with a dimple and always dresses so nice. If I weren't dead inside, that smile might make my heart flutter. Today, he's in a gray suit and tie. When I smile back, I realize he's still standing there. *Does he want to talk to me?* My smile slips. We've never said more than a few words to each other. Quickly, I grin again and motion for him to come in.

"Hey, how was Thanksgiving?" Logan says.

"Um, good. Yours?" The silence in my head will surely smother me.

He sets a plate down on my desk and sits in the spare chair without me motioning toward it. *Is he here to hang out?* Now I'm a little on edge.

"It was good. Got to see a lot of my family, so that was nice. I grew up here, so I have relatives all over the city. Did you visit family?"

"No. I went to a friend's Thanksgiving at her parents' house. My parents aren't here anymore, and my brother is out of town. It was nice, though." I play with the blue-green beaded bracelet I'm wearing, spinning it around my wrist.

"Aw, I'm sorry to hear that about your parents."

"Excuse me?"

"You said they aren't here—"

"Oh." Gah! "No, my mom and stepdad moved to Florida, and my dad is in Seattle. They are all alive and well, just not living in the area anymore."

"That's great that your friend invited you to join her family. Do you do that often?"

"I've met them a few times." Despite my best efforts to maintain my anti-social energy barrier, I feel it starting to come down. Logan is nice to talk to. "One of our other friends joined us too, since her parents are out of the country."

"That's really nice. The people of Pittsburgh are so friendly. My family welcomed in a couple of my roommates for holidays back when I was in college, and I know lots of other people who have done the same thing. That's one of the reasons I don't think I could leave this place."

"It's definitely special." I glance back at my computer, sure I should get back to my work.

Logan must have noticed because he sits forward in the chair and gestures at the plate on my desk. "Well, I know you're busy, but I stopped by because I wanted to make sure you got some banana bread. I baked it over the weekend, and I know you tend to stay in your office most of the day when you're not on site. Didn't want you to miss out."

"Oh. I appreciate it, but I'm good. I ate before I came in."

"Do you want a piece for later?"

Of course he would offer that. "Thank you, but not really."

"Ah." Logan seems disappointed, hopefully not offended. "It was nice talking to you anyway. I'll see you later." He scoops up the plate and smiles at me. It is a hard-to-read smile. Seems friendly, maybe offended. I'm sure that I'm constantly secretly offending people, especially when I turn down food.

"I'll see ya. Thanks again for stopping by." I smile and grasp for something to say to smooth things over. "Hey, by the way ... I like your tie." I actually do. It's deep blue and covered in a pattern of gingerbread boys and girls.

He glances down and grabs the tie, as if he forgot what he was wearing. "Thanks! I like to get festive early."

"Same here. See you later." I turn back to my computer as he leaves. Breathing out slowly, I frown. I sip my coffee. Man, I hate doing that. Just hope the guy isn't offended.

I notice that he hovers for a moment outside the door and then heads in the direction of the break room, probably to drop off the bread for everyone else. I feel bad, but I need to work. That was nice though! I should probably talk to my coworkers a little more often and about more than just work-related things. Maybe this is the dawn of a new Kenzi.

I'll think about it.

Chapter 2

I've always wanted to run an architectural design firm like Baker & Willow, and I hope to do that someday. I love the idea of being at the top of my game and having a team that I love that also loves what we do. *Love, love, love*, right? Sounds fun to love my life that much!

But things are good the way they are.

For now, Baker & Willow is perfect. Miranda Baker, one of the owners, has been an amazing mentor to me for the past few years. She encourages me to trust my gut ... and I really don't know where to go with that. I try. (I know, there is no *try*. Only *do*.) But it's hard. I know it's been a while, but I prefer to just get approval on my designs. I like passing it to another designer who checks it to make sure it all works. I feel like I need that little bit of reassurance. So, for now, I'm just going to keep getting my gold stars and see how I feel about opening myself up to ... trust.

Which is why my meeting with Miranda today is a little unsettling ...

"Kensington," she says my name like it's her favorite type of ice cream. And Miranda is the only person who calls me by my real name. She thinks it's stylish and that I should use it professionally. It somehow feels clunky though, like I still need to grow into it. "You're an excellent designer. I love how you focus on green products to help our clients meet their goals, which makes me especially proud of all the LEED-certified projects that you've led." Miranda leans forward and crosses her arms on her desk. She always does this before the other shoe drops. Her gold bracelets clink together as she moves. Her cropped navy tweed jacket looks stiff and formal against them, but the ivory dress she's wearing beneath makes her skin and strawberry blonde hair glow. I feel tiny and sloppy suddenly in her presence.

I feel like I'm shrinking into myself right now. But I also want to chuckle about the phrasing of the "LEEDs that I led." LEEDs are my favorite, of course, since that means the buildings include sustainable materials and practices. Gotta love Mother Earth! I take a deep breath and focus on the photo of the Pittsburgh skyline above her desk, a popular shot by Kira Claremont. I LOVE Miranda. I can't ask for a better boss and mentor. But good grief, why is she looking at me like that?

"The truth is, though, I know you've been hiding behind your team."

Now I'm really confused. "What do you mean? We need our team."

"You always ask for people to double-check you. You talk about a design and wait for someone to say it's a good idea. You ask me about things instead of just pushing ahead and doing the work like you believe in yourself. You treat me like a teacher rather than a peer."

"Are you saying I lack confidence?"

"I think so." Miranda paused. "I'm not complaining. You're very talented. I want you to stretch yourself though. When I put you in charge of a project, I want you to really lead."

I bite my lip. *Yeah, I've noticed this stuff too*, I thought. But I've only been at this a few years! How long do you have to do a thing to know like you know like you know that you have mastered that thing?

"Kenzi, I don't want you to worry. I'm just pushing you a little. I want you to be sitting here where I am someday, and I need you to start being the leader that you are. I can see her inside of you."

My eyes got wide.

"Are you OK?"

"Oh. No. I'm not dying or anything."

Miranda gave a short laugh and shook her head. "Look. I've been working with you for several years, and I see your potential. I want you to grow through the ranks here, lead the team, and know that you really are good at what you do. Stop second guessing yourself."

"I see. I'll work harder."

She gives me a sympathetic look. "You're missing the point. It's not a 'work harder' thing. It's a belief that you are truly the best person to do the job that you are doing right now and that you are doing it to the best of your ability."

I'm still a little confused. I bite my lip. "What do you recommend, then?"

"I read this book recently, and I think it will help you." She picks up the copy of *Trusting Your Superpowers* by Jennifer Halliday that was lying on her desk.

I take the book and stare at the cover. A beautiful woman in all white is staring powerfully directly into my eyes—it feels like the Mona Lisa times ten—with a red scarf billowing around her, giving the idea of a cape. The colors of the setting sun grace the background. A book is going to help? "Thanks. I'll start on it immediately."

"Good. I think that will help you start predicting new clients' needs. Trusting your intuition. You're at that point in your career now."

"It's as easy as that?" I laugh.

Miranda smiles and walks around her desk, so I stand. "Read the book first. I think it will make a difference. You have some goals now for the next few months."

"Sounds good. Thanks for the talk." I pick up the book from my lap and head toward the door.

"Oh, and one more thing. Are you familiar with Divya Shanti?"

"Yes! I love her. Clean lines. Bold colors. Plenty of sheen. My favorite purse is from her collection a couple years ago."

"Right. The purse with the orchids on it?" Miranda's eyes sparkle. I nod. "They are moving their headquarters to Pittsburgh and just signed with us to design the building—"

"That's amazing! I'm sure it will be a cool project to handle!"

"I'd like you to head up the project, starting in January." Miranda smiles gently at me, like she knows this is a huge gift ... rather than a panic-inducing anvil on my head.

"Me?" I squeak.

"It's right up your alley."

I'm pretty sure I'm making a face, which prompts Miranda to respond. "It won't be anything like St. Gregory's."

We both laugh.

St. Gregory's wasn't a disaster, per se, but it was certainly ... interesting. I designed a new church for the St. Gregory's congregation after a fire destroyed their previous home. You're probably thinking, "Holy smokes!" but they didn't have a sense of humor about it or really about anything, which made them a little tough to work with. I was already nervous because it was one of my first projects to lead, and they wavered between "fire and brimstone" and "holier than thou" in their responses to any of my questions.

It didn't help that a sinkhole from an abandoned oil drilling site, or as they call it in the industry a "legacy well," opened up where we planned to put their new parking lot. Thank God no one was hurt. Of course, they *did* thank Him. And we were all grateful. And then, against my better judgment, and prompted by my nerves, I made a joke that they could always put a sign in front of it that said, "The Pits of Hell," which may increase church attendance, and I nearly got glared off the lot.

We managed to address the sinkhole, save the church, and finish the whole project without any other incidents. Or bad jokes on my part. Again, thank God.

Moments after my visit with Miranda, I sit down in my desk chair and look around. The soft gray walls of my office feel cozy. Over my credenza, the bold watercolor of salsa dancers in the middle of a street relaxes me. This is my space, here.

I can absolutely do this. Step up in my career. Plan Christmas dinner. Design Divya Shanti's flipping headquarters. This is what it's like to be an adult, right? I'm totally there. I'm old enough. Right? Geez. Why do I still feel like a kid? Gray hairs, hello?

But it's all on me!

I look at the book in my hand. *Trusting Your Superpowers*. The author assumes that we all have superpowers then? Or maybe just the people brave enough to read this book.

Breathing in deeply, I know what I have to do. First off, calm the F down. Second, I need to read this book. I can figure the rest out from there. I know that I can at least trust *Miranda's* superpowers, and if she thinks I should read this book, I'll read it.

It's funny that she said she can see me sitting in her chair someday. Running the show. That's something I want. To get there from here, I suppose I better do everything she suggests.

But ... that little feeling in my stomach returns again. *Leave. Run away.* If I jump jobs, maybe change cities, then I will be too new for people to trust with the really big stuff like this. Maybe I can coast. Hide. It's a feeling like ants crawling across my organs. I want to leave, but I love people here. What if this is really a good place for me? What if I need to keep pushing forward in my career? What if Miranda really is training me to take over someday?

Do I want that?

After what happened last year, when my whole life was wrecked ... the familiar desire to run feels like a warm, wooly blanket, and I want to wrap myself in it and lose myself to its depths.

A new place? Starting over for real? Putting my past behind me?

I sigh. Maybe a conversation for when I'm not freaking out.

I place the book on my desk and turn back to my projects for the afternoon.

———

After work, as I pace around my house, starting this new project is the only thing on my mind. I know I can pull this off. I know that my career depends on it.

I walk into my cozy bedroom and flop on the bed. Breathe. Divya Shanti! This is going to work, right? I'm going to need my most comfortable loungewear for it. I grab my favorite knit pants and matching top—ha, they are *not* black—they are deep purple. And I head to the office in my spare bedroom.

This is the best thinking space. With a window into the peaceful backyard, a small flat-ish area, rare for this part of Pennsylvania, the lighting is gentle, allowing in the glow of the setting sun. I tip the blinds and sit at the desk by the window, journal ready, book open.

I can take notes on my superpowers and figure out what to do based on ... whatever Ms. Halliday says in her book.

A pair of cardinals flits across the lawn and lands in the huge oak at the corner of the yard. Most of the leaves have fluttered from the tree over the last month, but a few still cling on, shaking in the breeze. Soon, the cardinals slip away to another part of the yard, where the holly bushes hold tight with their deep green and bright red berries giving pops of color to an otherwise dull landscape.

In my journal, I start to sketch the cardinals in the yard by the holly. Then I stop. Yeah, I gotta read this book ...

Leaning back in the chair, I observe the room around me. Like the rest of the house, it's painted Swiss Coffee, white with a tinge of brown for warmth. Sometimes when one of my parents visits, they stay in this room, so the bed has a welcoming gray comforter with emerald green throw pillows. A painting of a pine forest in the mountains hangs above the bed for winter. In the spring, I will replace it with an image by a local painter of a path with huge sprawling deciduous trees and wildflowers that I just took down in October.

In the post-Thanksgiving coziness, though, something is missing—and it's distracting. I'm not going to get anything done till I get some Christmas decorations up. It's definitely time to get full-on festive!

I close the book and my journal. Then I go to my two-stall garage, where part of the second stall is filled with huge Rubbermaid bins. Declan always likes to joke that I've never seen a Christmas decoration I didn't like.

He's right.

I lug six bins to the living room to start on the tree and décor. Then, I jog to the kitchen to warm up some leftover pizza for dinner. "Alexa, play the album *Warmer in the Winter*." The strains of Lindsey Stirling's violin playing "Dance of the Sugarplum Fairy" burst through the speaker, and I traipse back to the living room with my cauliflower crust pizza.

By the time I'm assembling the tree, the Grinch song starts playing, and I'm lost in the music, shaking my booty and jamming while I flare the branches apart. The lights take a little longer, of course, because I like to add so many strands that my tree looks like it's on fire. Halfway through the album, I'm a slice of pizza down, and the tree is covered in tasteful silver and red balls.

I open another box of ornaments and see all the sentimental ones from over the years: my "baby's first Christmas" ornament from all those years ago, the glass violin from when I made the all-state orchestra my senior year of high school, and cutout ornaments in lots of Christmas shapes from when my college roommates and I were "elfing" and making festive, cheap presents for everyone we knew. I add them all to the tree. Near the bottom of the box, though, I find one that always gives me pause.

I went through a strange crafting phase in middle school where I wanted to make things that would last, but not out of Popsicle sticks or clay. My mother got me plastic canvas and yarn from the craft store, and I spent hours making my creations. My little cousin got a bed for her Barbie's baby. My dad got a picture frame for the desk in his office. For myself, I made a house. I cut up the canvas, making intricate rooflines, a portico, and an odd octangular room at the corner of the house. I put a lot of work into the little house, especially stitching through all the canvas with yarn. It has hung on my tree since that year.

Seeing that, I scoop it up and sit on the couch for a moment, reminiscing about what a 12-year-old was feeling that would lead her to such an intricate project. I was always pretty mature for my age, but this was more than maturity. This was the desire to create something beautiful that lived in my head. I was breathing it into being.

Smiling, I hang it front and center on the tree and retreat to the kitchen for a second slice of pepperoni. Returning to the living room, I tuck ribbon around the tree and place a huge silver snowflake at the top when my phone buzzes.

Come outside.

It's my neighbor, Lauren, who rents the other half of the duplex from me. Why not? I grab a coat and gloves and slip them on as I walk out the front door.

By now, the sun has set, when what to my wondering eyes should appear but ... a whole herd of shiny, light-up reindeer.

"I couldn't resist! I bought them today. *They were on sale!*" Lauren wears a bright turquoise wool coat with a cream knitted scarf and matching hat and looks like she has simply called the reindeer to join her on the lawn for a picnic. She is an ethereal being with her angular, elfin face, slim body, and long auburn locks.

"How did you get them all here? Do you have carrots in your pocket?"

She smiles her gleaming grin and exaggerates a flip of her hair over her shoulder. "I asked Leo, down the street, if I could borrow his truck."

"Who? Wait, *you* drove a truck?"

"No no. I asked if he would come to pick something up for me, and we loaded his truck together. He was a big help." Lauren pauses and admires her new Christmas décor. "You need to meet more people in the neighborhood. You never know when you'll need a hand or can help them out with something."

I glance sideways at the deer, which will apparently be part of our Christmas menagerie this year ... adding to the gingerbread house cutouts for our porticos that match the gingerbread people standing in front of the pillars—all of which Lauren surprised me with last week right before Thanksgiving. Her brother helped her install them.

"You're one of those fun 'roommates,' aren't you?"

"The best kind, my dear!" Lauren links arms with me and gazes wide-eyed at our duplex. "What else do we need? I'm kind of excited to get started decorating the outside with you."

Cackling, I gaze at her like she's crazy. "We need *more*?"

"Yes! Lights! More lights! Oh, and garland for the pillars. And lights and ornaments on the oak. And maybe some wreaths on the windows."

"And a partridge in a pear tree?"

"Don't be silly. This is an *oak* tree." She points at the large oak in the front yard. "Maybe just some icicle lights across the gutters and something for the mailboxes and the light posts. What did you put up last year?"

Again, I laugh, a sour one this time. "A wreath on the front door. I wasn't exactly in the mood after Thomas."

Lauren winces. "True. Well, that's all changing this year ... for both of us. Christmas is the time to light up the world!"

"You'll have to slow down a bit. I'm just starting on the inside!"

She winks at me. "That's a good place to start."

Chapter 3

A short time later, Lauren and I are in her living room, seated on her sleek pink vegan leather—fine, it's plastic—couch and sipping hot chocolate. I'm pouring out the stressors of the past 24 hours to her, and she's nodding respectfully, looking like she's ready to burst with all the solutions. I'm totally not ready to hear how she can just whisk in with her magic wand and reframe all the stress so that now it's all a bunch of opportunities.

But it's *stress*ful, dammit. And I'm freaking out. And that's comfortable for me. So I languish in my panic-mode, nibbling some salt and vinegar chips that Lauren and I LOVE, and snuggle under one of the faux fur throws draped over all of Lauren's furniture. Her living room is boho chic and, thanks to winter, now has tons of snuggly, *hygge* accents—I think that's the word she used—the Danish word for "cozy" and "content" and "soul-level perfection" or something. Between the plants, blankets, pillows, and her Christmas tree and knickknacks, it's pretty packed in here, which I suppose is Lauren's definition of cozy.

Her Monet's *Water Lilies* poster from summer was replaced mid-October with a simple poster with a geometric image of a winter sunset over the mountains, a river meandering in the foreground.

The pillows and throws pick up the colors of the poster beautifully, and her tree even coordinates. It's so comforting being in an environment created by someone who has the same level of attention to detail that I do with architecture. It's good to hang out with artists!

But back to the issue at hand ... "So basically, I'm expected to host Christmas for ten people, which I've never done, and read this book and become some '*next best version of me*' (according to the back of the book) so I can stop being a wienie at work and keep my bosses happy, and so I can take on potentially the biggest project of my lifetime in January: designing the new HQ for Divya Shanti.

Lauren, as usual, is sipping her hot matcha latte thoughtfully, nodding in sympathy, but definitely concocting a plan to make me feel better, which is potentially the best trait in a best friend. "I don't know what to tell you. That's a lot."

I'm sorry, what?

"You're not going to tell me how to feel better and make the most of it and reframe and yadda yadda from the latest self-help guru you've been following?"

"Oh that. Yeah, I'm trying to have healthier boundaries and not solve everyone's problems for them. Sage is starting to rely heavily on me for that, and she really needs to have just some nudges in the right direction instead. Can't let a 13-year-old get out of the habit of working things out for herself." Sage is Lauren's niece, who stays over a lot because Lauren likes to help her sister Taylor out. She works a lot of extra hours as a single mom so she can pay for braces and put money aside for Sage to go to college and all that good stuff. Sage's teeth look great, but I'm sure it takes a toll.

"Sorry if I was relying on you for that too." My head was reeling. What if she's just letting me hang out because she feels bad for me? *Oh my God, I'm a charity case!*

"No worries," Lauren laughs. "I'll give you a nudge, just like I'm trying to do with Sage." She sat up straighter, sipped her drink, and then gave me a wise look. "So, what do you think you need most right now to help you believe in yourself?"

"Believe in myself?"

"Yes, because it sounds like a lot of great opportunities—" Ha! "—and I'm sure that your stress is coming from a lack of belief in yourself to handle all these fabulous things. Which is probably something that Miranda spotted too, since she gave you that book to level up."

"So does the matcha latte make you wise?"

"Lots of personal development. I've been following Ashley Lewis on all her social, and she gives the best tips. Her book, *All About the Good Karma,* is life-changing."

"I'll add it to my list." Good grief, I'm behind.

"You know what else might help you change your perspective?" Lauren paused to let me answer, but I didn't. I had no idea what to say. "Changing your physical position on this planet."

"I'm not doing another cleanse with you."

"What? No. I mean moving around. Getting out of town. Going on vacation."

That is actually appealing. "But I don't want to go anywhere by myself."

"First off, traveling by yourself is so freeing. You don't have to compromise with anyone about where to go, you can eat and go to the bathroom whenever you want, and you don't have to take care of anyone. So. Freeing. Just you and the world."

"That sounds like a really enlightened way of saying 'lonely.'"

"Are you lonely in your house?"

"No."

"Then how could you be lonely when you're spending your time how you want, seeing what you want, and indulging yourself a little. 'Alone' isn't 'lonely.'"

She's right. Crap. "OK, you're right. But I don't know where I would even go."

"How about Rome?"

"Like in Italy?"

"Sure."

I snort laugh. "You want me to fly to Rome by myself?"

"Do you have a passport?"

"I do, but—"

"Yay!" Lauren sets her mug down and lunge-hugs me. "OK, I've been bursting to tell you about this."

My eyes, about as big around as the peppermint throw pillow I've been hugging, stare at her. I suddenly snap out of it and return the hug right before she lets go and flops back to the couch. My face clearly says *well, what?* when I can't express it with words.

"Do you remember the wedding I did last summer for Gianmarco Zangari's daughter?"

How could I forget? Lauren designed a wedding dress and the bridesmaids' dresses for the daughter of a famous leather coat and shoe designer based in Italy. The wedding was held in Boston at some ritzy, gorgeous venue. I loved the pictures; the building was truly amazing. Oh, and the décor too, but let's be honest, my heart is with the building. At the wedding, everyone got a pair of leather loafers from the designer, and they are only the most comfortable, buttery soft leather shoes I've ever seen. And worn. I borrow Lauren's whenever she will let me (thank God we wear the same size shoes), and she's wearing them now, a beautiful forest green. I glance at her feet and then back to her eyes, which are about the same color. "Yeah?"

"He has a villa outside of Rome near Castel Gandolfo ... and I've stayed in touch with his wife, Ottavia, since the wedding. She is such a sweet woman. Oh, and she referred me to her friend for a design this spring. Did I show you the dress I did for her?"

"You did ... but tell me about the villa. Is it really old? Do they do tours?" Do I want to go to Rome to tour a villa? Alone?

"The villa is gorgeous. I saw some pictures when Ottavia was showing me their Christmas decorations last winter. Just beautiful." Then she adds all sing-songy, "You would love it ..." which made me wonder again if I really want to go to Italy and see this place. Maybe I could do a tour of just architecture. Do normal people do that?

Do I want to be normal?

"I'd love to see pictures," I finally say. Because I really would. It would probably be lovely.

"How about something better than pictures?" Lauren sits up straighter again, like she is ready to present a proposal. I hold up my hands like I want her to just spit it out. "So, Ottavia told me that they were going to put an event venue on their property. They often hold shows for their new collections and do big events in the Rome area for various reasons, but they wanted it to be more convenient and less cost-prohibitive. If it's on their property, they don't have to worry about booking a place, AND they don't have to worry about parking people in Rome and getting directions out and all the other stuff you normally have to deal with."

"I'm not sure what you're getting at." My stomach suddenly flutters. "Do they need an architect?" What if I could fly to Rome to help design a building? And then I shuddered when I realized the insane amount of pressure I would be under.

"Good guess, but no. Sorry. Don't be sad." Lauren pats my arm. "As they were digging for the foundation, they ran into some ... stuff. Antiques? What do you call that stuff? Like floor tiles, bones, pottery shards. A lot of old stuff." She gestures vaguely.

"Artifacts? Relics?" I suggest. "It sounds pretty cool. Are they going to let people see what they find?"

"Yeeessssss ... they actually need people to help find it. They had to stop digging the foundation and brought in a team of archeologists. It's now a dig into ancient Rome! It's pretty exciting. And the archeologists said that Ottavia and Gianmarco could ask for volunteers to join them, that way it goes faster. They can see if there is anything important there, and they may be able to get back on track quickly."

"Oh, how cool!" I'm still not sure why she's telling me all of this.

"Soooooo ... do you want to go with me? I just found out about the dig over the weekend, and I have been thinking about it. I want to do this. I mean, when will I get another chance to find ancient artifacts? The most we ever dig up in this part of the world is an arrowhead or the one horseshoe you said you found when they were working on Chestnut Acres."

"And sometimes bricks and nails from previous builds."

"Right, but nothing with *history*. Nothing that feels really weighty. Can you imagine? We could go to the outskirts of Rome and actually be walking where people walked like two thousand years ago."

"Maybe we can have a Caesar salad for lunch."

"You're ridiculous." Lauren sipped her latte.

"But don't they only eat pasta there?"

"That's racist."

"No it isn't! I'm part Italian. And it's a legitimate concern!"

"We can figure out food while we're there. Ottavia will help us." Lauren waits for another objection and then says, "So what do you think?"

"It sounds ... interesting." Is this my thing? I'm used to museums, but actually digging for the stuff they put there? Like, all Indiana Jones? Probably more dirty. Less glamorous. Definitely without being chased by bad guys or hot romances along the way. "It's hard to say. What are the details?"

"Three weeks in Italy, December 1–22. Ottavia said we can stay at their villa. There will be 16 volunteers total. I asked Macy if she wanted to come and bring her boyfriend, but they have a trip planned already. Everyone signed up is connected to the family, so they are all vetted. No weirdos. No one random—"

"You can't guarantee that they won't be weirdos. Just potentially safe weirdos."

"True, but the family is personally inviting people, not putting it up on Eventbrite or anything. So 'no one random' is a guarantee."

"But what if we don't get along with the other people on the dig? That's a long time to be stuck with people you don't like!"

"Why would you even think that?"

"I'm nervous around my coworkers."

"But they are fine, right? It's not that you don't like them. You just don't know them."

"I guess you're right. Continue."

"So, they have eight rooms for volunteers to stay at the villa—"

"How big is this place?"

"Like big. I think she said they have ten bathrooms. And they want people to come in pairs, like a couple or two friends, so they can pair up with the bedrooms and not have strangers staying together."

"That makes sense. So, this will be like that retreat you talked me into over the summer except we will be doing manual labor and won't know what anyone is saying to us."

"When you put it that way, it sounds way less fun." Lauren grins. "Are you in?"

"We would only have three days to get everything cleared, pack, and go. I'll have to talk to Miranda about it tomorrow. I have the vacation time and my passport." Glad we crossed into Canada when I went to Niagara Falls with my ex last summer ...

"I'm wrapping up a wedding dress and bridesmaid dresses for a winter wedding with crimson accents this week. Our final fittings are tomorrow, so I'm almost done. The timing to escape is perfect."

"You don't have to be at the wedding, right?"

"Nope." Lauren shifts on the couch and covers up with a soft green furry blanket. "We just have to book flights, which could be a little nutty. Ottavia said she could help us. She has connections."

I realize that I've been sitting on the edge of the couch, anticipating how this couldn't possibly work out because, honestly, it sounds pretty exciting, like a neat chance to escape, relax, recalibrate. But it should work. There isn't really a reason I wouldn't be able to go. It sounds pretty safe, I have the time to take off, and really, I could use a vacation. "Oh no. What about planning Christmas?"

"I'll help you. I don't think it will be as hard as you are making yourself believe it will be."

I blink a couple times as this new reality sets in. "Then I guess we're going to Rome!"

Lauren grabs me again and squeezes me like a boa constrictor. "Eeeee! I'm so excited." She whips out her phone. "I'm going to email Ottavia now and have her reserve our spots. We're going to Rome!"

Chapter 4

The next day at work, I know I have to talk to Miranda about going on the trip. I'm a little nervous, but I think she will go for it and actually encourage me. She wants me to spread my wings, to learn and grow. Surely, she will see the benefits and tell me to hop on that plane.

I'm wearing my favorite fuchsia silk blouse and Divya Shanti crystal pave dangly earrings to give me some extra confidence today.

I slip into the break room and beeline to the coffee pot to top off my coffee and warm it up—geez, it's freezing in the 'burgh today—and then head to Miranda's office. I tap on her doorframe, since the door is open, and she smiles, motioning for me to come in.

"Hey, Kensington."

I'm not sure how to broach this, so I sit down, sigh, and just start talking, hoping I say it right. "I wanted to talk to you about something." Good start. Obvious. Keep going. She raises her perfectly plucked eyebrows. "I have a really interesting opportunity, and I'd like to take three weeks off for it. In December."

"Wow, what is it? I mean, you have the time. You're wrapping up the Bedford project right now, right?" She squints at her computer screen, likely bringing up the project board where we track everything. Then she nods in agreement with what she just said, her lob bouncing.

"A dig." That sounds ridiculous. "I'm going with my friend Lauren to Rome for a dig." Not much better. And she isn't saying anything. Oh no, I pissed her off. "It will be a great chance for me to study the architecture there ...?" Now I sound like I'm filling out a form for an excused absence from school for a trip to the beach.

"What do you mean by 'a dig'?" Her tone sounds like she's intrigued. I brief her on the details. "That sounds amazing! Of course, yes, I approve. I'll mark you as off. You're leaving on ... the first?"

"Yeah."

"That's just a couple days away. You'll have to pack quickly." Miranda gave me a proud big sister look. "I love that you're doing this. You're not usually so spontaneous, but I'm glad you decided to go. I hope you have a wonderful time."

A little nervous niggle works its way through my gut. "I hope so too."

"It's OK to have a good time." She looks closer at me. "You seem concerned. You don't have any reason to worry. We can handle things while you're gone. And you'll be refreshed and ready to start on the Divya Shanti building when you get back."

"Right," I say with way more conviction than I feel. Right.

I make my way back down the hall, around the corner, directly toward my office. I'm debating how best to tell Mom about the little hiccup in her holiday plans and also debating about when I should just sit down and come up with a menu. Then, with my head firmly in la la land, I nearly smack into Logan coming out of the break room with a little more holly jolly in his step than most people have at this time in the morning. I narrowly miss dumping my coffee on him, slipping my hand off to the side and by some miracle keeping all the coffee in the mug.

"Whoa. Sorry about that. I was just dropping off some cookies for everyone. Pizzelles, sugar cookies, chocolate peppermint swirls ... Make sure you pop in and grab some."

"Ah. I'll do that. Thank you," I am a little preoccupied, so I hope my dry response doesn't sound *too* dry. Honestly, I don't touch cookies that other people make because—

"Oh. What is your favorite kind of cookie?" I guess he picked up on my disappointment.

"I, uh—" My phone dings, though, and I don't have time to think about how to answer Logan. It's Mom.

Kenzi, can you let me know when you have the menu ready for Christmas Day? I want to help out the best I can. Stan and I can pick up ingredients and come early to make something. Whatever you need, Sweetie!

I swear she knows I am thinking about the menu.

"Sorry, Logan, it's my mom. It's important." I start texting as I'm standing by my office door, the slick "Kenzi B. Ashbury, RA" nameplate by my elbow, juggling my coffee and the phone, and looking the opposite of slick. "Hey Mom, I was just—" Then I realize that I could just put the coffee down. It's not an emergency. Mom can wait two minutes while I get situated.

But before I can set down the mug, I hear Logan say my name.

Turning, I nearly drop my phone in the coffee and end up splashing the coffee on the wall and floor as I jump back to avoid getting it all over me.

"Everything OK?" Logan says. He jumps back just in time too.

"No, there should be a 'splash zone' sign near me like they have by dolphin tanks." I stare at the mess for a moment and thank the Lord that my phone didn't go in the coffee and that I didn't get coffee on Logan. Yes, in that order.

"Let me help." Logan jogs back to the kitchen and returns with a roll of paper towels, while I set my coffee and phone on my desk.

"Thank you." I take the offered towels and mop up my hand and the floor while he wipes the wall. "Guess I only needed half a cup after all," I joke as I glance at the remainder of my coffee.

"I meant is your mom OK?" Logan points at my phone. "You looked worried."

"Oh, she's fine. Just asking about Christmas. I have to host this year. And I'm just ..." Why am I going into details? "Just realizing I thought I was more talented than I am and could text and walk with coffee at the same time."

"I get it. My family is already talking about Christmas too." He smiled knowingly. "I can grab you some more coffee if that will help."

I look at the screen and see a series of texts from my mom in response to my half text that I accidentally sent before the phone narrowly missed nose diving into java.

"Guess I already replied. I'll get to all her question marks in a minute. She can wait." I start walking back toward my office.

Logan says, "You'll have to let me know about the cookies. I plan on baking more this week." His hair is parted on the side, so it fell in his eyes when we were cleaning. He brushes it back, and I notice it looks thick and soft. It's almost the color of hazelnuts.

I snap back to focus. "Thank you!" I call, trying to sound warm and genuine. I did almost dump coffee on the guy twice.

As I head back to my office, my phone starts vibrating. It's Mom.

"Kenzi, you only texted part of a sentence, and then you didn't answer, so I got worried. Are you OK?"

"Mom, I'm fine." I pause as I shut my office door. "I just spilled some coffee and had to wipe it up before it stained the carpet." She would understand that. Mom hates stains.

"Oh, I hate stains." See? "I'm glad you cleaned that up first. Now about that menu ... did you add cookies to it? I know you don't eat them, but Declan's kids will want cookies. And Stan. Actually, everyone but *you* will want cookies—"

"Yes, cookies are on the list. Actually, that's all that's on the list so far, but I will take care of it. I promise." Cookies like ones I can actually eat ...

"That's good. We can pick some up if you need us to when we get to town. I know you're at work, so I'll let you go. Stan and I are on our way to the beach anyway, so we will be busy for the next few hours. It's gorgeous here!"

I shiver, acknowledging the chilly (roughly freezing) temps in Pittsburgh. "Glad you're having fun, Mom! Tell Stan I said hi."

"I will. Byeeee!"

"Bye."

Drumming my hands on the desk, I gaze off for a moment after I hang up. Honestly, I have plenty of time to come up with a menu. It shouldn't be a problem.

———

Cori Wamsley

Grandma Claudia is one of the few family members I have left in the area, so I make a point of visiting her, getting her groceries, and taking her out when I can. After work, I drive north to pick her up at her cottage and take her to Phipps Conservatory, a beautiful greenhouse and botanical garden that features different art installations throughout the year. This year, Francoise Bourdillon's Nutcracker Ballet-inspired metal sculptures are scattered throughout the gardens, and Grandma mentioned that she would love to see them. I told her to dress warmly so we could meander through the displays and take our time.

As we walk into the first room, we are greeted with a burst of color from dozens of poinsettias, the metal sculptures pirouetting through the flowers with graceful snowflake skirts. It really is breathtaking. Grandma and I approach the wall around the garden and examine the little metal ballerinas. Such exquisite detail!

The next room is full of long sword-like plants with rat sculptures, less of a favorite, but I still appreciate the artistic talent it took to create the rats. Then we enter a room with a waterfall, the Sugar Plum Fairy cascading through the waters and a gingerbread land gracing the grounds.

A short time later, we find ourselves by the café and grab mugs of hot chocolate.

"This is lovely, but I definitely need a break," Grandma says. "I hope you're finding some inspiration for your next project here."

"This is purely for enjoyment, Grandma." I sip my hot cocoa slowly. It tastes like drinking a chocolate bar. "I don't start the next project till January." I pause, wondering how she's going to take the next bit of news. "I'm going to Italy for three weeks, starting on the first of December."

You would think that the actual rat king just walked into the room. "Italy? This time of year? What for? Do you need money?"

"What? No, Grandma, I don't need money. What does that have to do with going to Italy?"

"I was offering to help. Did you think I was asking if that's why you're going?" Grandma laughs heartily.

Now I'm a little embarrassed. Of course she was offering to help. Grandma doesn't question my judgment. She just wants to make sure I reach my goals. "I did. Sorry about that. But no, I don't need any money. I already paid for my ticket." I brief her on the dig.

"I think this will be good for you." Grandma smiles and warms her hands on the mug. "You grew up inspired by everything, especially LEED and green design. That's why I thought you wanted to bring me to Phipps."

"No, I know how much you love *The Nutcracker*. That's why we came."

"I know. You're really selfless. I hope that while you're in Italy, you take a step back and just enjoy it. Don't worry about it becoming part of your work. Just let it be. Breathe it in. If it's meant to inspire you, it will seep into your veins, and you'll bring it back. If not, it will just be a wonderful experience. Don't think too hard about it or try to make it something that it isn't."

I frown. Do I really do that with everything? Does everything need a purpose?

Just then, my phone dings. Mom texts me about whether we need a charcuterie board. "It's Mom." She's looking at one in a store. I don't know! Do we need that? Can I just use my medium platter? I know my eyebrows are doing facial gymnastics as I think of what to say. I don't get to make decisions like this, like ever. I respond—

Whatever you like!

Grandma smirks. "Is it about Christmas?" I nod. "I thought it would be. That's all she thinks about from Thanksgiving on!" She chuckled. "I don't care what we have. I just want a boozy dessert."

"Hey! Can we join you?" Miranda and her husband are suddenly standing beside our table, holding hot cocoa, too.

"Sure!" I introduce them to Grandma Claudia. It's been a while since I've seen Miranda's husband, so I'm hoping that his name is Brad, as I introduce him as such.

"I'm Brent." The not-Brad extends his hand to shake Grandma's. Oh no. I'm terrible. How could I screw that up? But Miranda doesn't seem to notice. Or maybe she doesn't care. I still feel awful.

"We were just talking about the new clubhouse that we're installing in Chestnut Acres," Miranda says. "The design reminds me of Phipps."

"You're right. I hadn't thought of that."

"Didn't you design some of the houses there too?" Brent says.

"I did," I answer, "but what's funny is that I didn't know I would actually be living there when I did it."

"Oh really? When did you end up buying your place?"

"A little over a year ago. I, uh ..." Probably best not to get discuss the messy breakup with my boss's husband. "Things lined up just right, and I was able to buy my duplex. I rent the other half to a woman who I've become great friends with."

"That's so amazing," Miranda jumps in. She pulls her navy wool wrap coat around her tighter. "That's honestly one of the reasons I got into architecture to begin with. I love that a building can bring people together. Everything I design has a story behind it. Sometimes, the story is even part of my process. I'll imagine the type of people using the space in the future, how they interact there, what they will be doing ... it makes for a really immersive design experience."

Brent stares at Miranda like he's falling in love with her all over again. A smile breaks across my face. To have that type of love ...

"This is something that never gets old," Brent says. He wraps his arm around Miranda. "I just love that she's so passionate about her work."

Suddenly, I feel like a bit of a third wheel, even with Grandma there. I think Grandma picks up on the vibe.

"Kenzi, I don't want to stay out too late." Grandma looks at Miranda and Brent. "It was so nice to meet you, but I really want to finish seeing everything here before it's my bedtime."

Miranda cuddled closer to Brent as we walked toward the last couple rooms.

Chapter 5

November 30th is a whirlwind.

The weather in Rome is normally in the 40s and 50s in December, so I know a puffer jacket and gloves will be important. But the forecast looks like it will be closer to 50s and 60s for the coming month, so I'll want some lighter jackets and jeans. And clothes to dig in. And possibly rain gear. And ...

I finally wonder if I should just pack everything I own.

Will I need any formal wear? A razor? I know I'll be in the dirt a lot, but I'm staying at a fancy villa, so ... eh?

When I've finally narrowed it down, I have a carryon, bag to check, and my Divya Shanti tote with the stripe of snowflakes around the bottom. And I only brought three novels with me. In the carryon because #priorities.

Our friend Macy offered to drop us off at the airport, so I pop over to Lauren's half of the duplex with my luggage when I'm ready.

I ring the doorbell and wait. Where is she?

"Kenzi, is that you?"

I turn and see Logan grinning at me. He's walking his dog, a big chocolate lab with a lolling tongue, on the main road. Since our house is on the corner, he easily saw me on the porch.

"Oh hey." I wave, thinking he will keep going, but he turns down our road and walks up the driveway.

"Are you staying here this weekend?" He bends and rubs the dog's head for a moment. "I'm down in the apartments on the next road."

"Nice. This is a good place to walk." Why hasn't Lauren answered her door? "Actually, this is my duplex, and my friend—" I gesture at the door, "— and I are leaving for a trip."

Of course, he asks where I'm going, and I explain briefly. He frowns as he listens to my explanation and then nods, smiling again. "Sounds like an amazing experience. Three weeks, huh? Long time to be gone, especially when you have to get everything ready for Christmas."

I bristle. "I think I'll be fine. As long as I have a boozy dessert, my grandma will be happy, and my brother's kids want cookies. Who's going to argue if Grandma and the kids are happy?"

"Solid point."

"Right!" I suddenly remember that Grandma's request didn't make it to the list, and I start digging in my bag for my phone. "I definitely don't want to forget. I need to add them to my—"

"Hey!" Breathless, Lauren bursts through her front door, shaking the wreath and causing the bells on it to jingle maniacally. "I am SO sorry. I was on the phone with Sage and didn't even hear you—" She pauses and glances from Logan to me, back to Logan, and then the dog. "Hi, I'm Lauren." She holds out her hand.

"Logan." He shakes her hand and then gestures to the dog. "Bacon."

Lauren and I both laugh. I refrain from snorting, which is good for me, because that's a pretty hilarious name for a dog. Lauren squats beside Bacon and rubs the inside of his ears with her fists. Then she breaks out the cutesy pet voice. "You have the funniest doggy name I've ever heard, but I just wuv you."

Bacon drools and squeezes his eyes shut with glee.

Logan chuckles warmly. "He's named after his favorite food. I was picking up my lunch when I first met him. He bounded right up to me in the parking lot and sniffed at my bag, so I sacrificed the bacon from my sandwich. He was a skinny little guy then." He strokes Bacon's now healthy back lovingly. "So, you guys are heading out?"

"As soon as my friend gets here. She's mailing something to her brother—so she should be here soon. It's something that all her siblings are working on for their parents for Christmas. They have a tradition of working together on a surprise every year."

"That's really nice," Logan says. "Do you guys have any Christmas traditions?"

"My family likes to do new pajamas on Christmas Eve," Lauren says. "I have about a million pairs of Christmas pjs now, but my favorites are the elf ones with the striped bottoms."

"Those are my favorites, too." I say.

"What about you Kenzi?"

"Besides the tree and Christmas dinner, not really. Mom and Dad split when we were little, and Dad moved to Seattle, the only city that possibly has more rain than Pittsburgh. Then, it was just Mom, Declan, and me for a long time. Then Declan sort of took over as the 'man of the house.'" I use air quotes to make sure they know I'm joking. "Mom remarried when I was in college. They moved to

Florida when they retired, so I don't see them a lot. And Declan and his family live across town, but right now, they are in Paris, so ..."

I pause for a second because I got a bit off track. "Anyway, Mom, Declan, and I used to go to Aunt Becky's for Christmas Eve dinner sometimes, but she moved to Florida too, a couple years ago, so right now it's just me in the 'burgh ... and a few cousins I'm not super close to and Grandma Claudia, who I see a lot." Lauren looks like she's about to say something, so I better wrap it up. "Sometimes one of my cousins has a Christmas party the week before Christmas, and I never miss it when it happens. Declan and his family always go too. Honestly, it's the only social event I look forward to. The only thing that makes it tolerable is that they are my family, even if we aren't close, like I said. It makes the whole *peopley* part bearable."

What am I saying? The look on Lauren's face clearly says that was a lot.

Logan doesn't seem to notice. "I think most people are like that. So many families have to split up the holidays with different parts of the family, husbands and wives. It makes it tough."

Just then, a tan Corolla pulls into the driveway and honks.

"There's Macy!" Lauren says. She grabs her suitcase, and I follow suit.

Macy hops from the driver's seat, her corkscrew curls bouncing with her, her fuchsia puffer stealing the show with the boldness of color in the bleakness of winter. She jogs over, hugs us, and grabs one of the big suitcases. Logan grabs the other.

We all load the trunk. That's a lot of luggage in her little car!

"You guys have fun! Send me a postcard!" Logan calls as we hop in the car. Bacon barks and wags his tail.

I pause as I'm sliding into the back seat. "I don't have your address."

"I'll email it to you."

———

I awaken to a cramped neck and the snoring of a bigger man sitting beside me. I'm pretty sure I saw him pop sleeping pills as we took off, and he's been out the entire flight. Lauren is blissfully jammed into the corner between her seat and the window, her head supported by a batik patterned neck pillow.

My belly jumps as we hit an air pocket during decent, and I grab the armrest. I too have slept most of the flight, and now I'm a bit nervous. I hate air pockets. I like smooth, bumpless flights. Or teleportation. Looking forward to that.

"Lauren. Almost there," I whisper to my seatmate.

With a snort, Lauren sits up and pops the ear plugs out of her ears. "Wow. I can't believe I slept the whole way.

I laugh. "I think I did too, but I definitely don't feel 'rested.'" I rub my neck for emphasis. I'll have to dig out some ibuprofen later if the kinks don't come out.

When we leave the luggage carousel, Lauren and I approach a gentleman holding a sign with our names, and he ushers us to a black Lincoln town car by the curb.

As we leave Leonardo da Vinci International Airport, I get bubbles of excitement in my stomach. I peer out the window, taking in the countryside. Italy's famous pines. Palms. Mountains. Ruins. God, it's amazing. We swing south of the city and turn off the highway, and quickly, I realize that I'm about to have a life-altering experience.

Partially because I'm certain we are about to die.

Our driver navigates the smaller roads like he really needs to get to the bathroom. It doesn't help that Vespas weave in and out of traffic like mosquitoes, regardless of whether the vehicles are stopped or moving.

I white-knuckle the armrest and wonder if the little bit of Italian I learned will help me tell the driver I'm getting car sick. I look at Lauren in desperation, but she is gazing between the seats to see out the front window and looks overjoyed.

"*Ci siamo quasi*," our driver calls.

Lauren shrugs and glances at me. I have no idea what he's saying. "You OK?"

My eyes bug as the car swerves into the turning lane and heads off toward Lago Albano. Lauren grabs my hand and squeezes. "You'll be OK in a sec." She points ahead.

The Zangari villa appears around a curve in the road behind a grove of Italy's iconic pines. A cream stucco two-story, the villa features a beautiful veranda wrapped around three sides with arched supports lined with stone. Terracotta tiles cover the roof in beautiful shades of spiced orange and brown. I could move in here purely because I'm in love with the architecture.

Our driver pulls into the brick drive and parks close to the front door. That's when I manage to tear my eyes from the building and notice the view.

The villa faces Lago Albano—a decent-sized lake—down the hill to the east, basking in the morning sun. It sparkles on the water like a gemstone. I step out of the car, my legs a little wobbly, my stomach still jittering. A gentle breeze stirs the pines and rustles the oleander and yellow may that line the drive.

This might be my new favorite place.

A couple enjoying morning coffee and cornettos on the front porch rise to greet us.

"Ciao Lauren, how wonderful to see you again!" the woman, wearing tan slacks and a black boat neck long-sleeve top, with a tan jacket thrown over her shoulders, approaches us. Her wavy hair is pinned on one side, streaks of gray mixing with the deep brown. She kisses Lauren on both cheeks and squeezes her hands. "And this is Kenzi?"

"Yes," I respond, shaking her hand. "So nice to meet you."

"I'm Ottavia, and this is my husband, Gianmarco." She gestures to the gentleman beside her. He's dressed stylishly, but casual, with a white linen shirt and loafers. A huge watch with a gold band glints on his wrist.

"A pleasure," Gianmarco says. He shakes hands with me and touches Lauren gently on the arm, smiling.

"Thank you for welcoming us to your beautiful home," Lauren says.

"You must be hungry. Please come in." Ottavia says. The nervous twitter from minutes before landing returns to my belly.

"Nico, please take their bags to the *Lavanda* room, *grazie*," Gianmarco says. To us, he comments. "*Lavanda* is 'lavender.' All the rooms have the names of flowers that grow in the Lago Albano region."

The couple escorts us into their home as Nico takes care of our luggage. I hope he's a little gentler with the turns with our bags than he was with the car.

The entranceway is gorgeous, of course. I gaze at the stucco walls with their brick and stone accents and frames for the open archway into the kitchen and living area. My eyes are drawn upward to the cathedral ceilings with dark chestnut rafters and exposed beams. Beautiful. I realize I'm staring and stopped walking, so I hurry to catch up to the rest of them as they enter the living area.

"Most of the volunteers came in last night," Ottavia was saying. "There are 16 total, sharing rooms in pairs. I thought you might meet some of them at breakfast, but I believe they are all still upstairs."

"I saw Alessia and Lena earlier. They are in the garden." Gianmarco gestures toward the open French doors off of the dining room. Beyond is an orchard of lemon trees surrounded by clumps of palms, oleander, and many more flowers. I can smell the sting of lemon mingling with the lift of floral perfume wafting in on the breeze. Heavenly.

"Oh good. They are your dig partners. Both are fluent in English, so I thought they would be able to help you with anything you need during the day. They are from the Firenze area. Florence." Ottavia stops by some platters on the counter piled high with *cornetti*, *biscotti*, and various *pane*—crescent rolls and breads. Homemade strawberry and peach jams are nearby.

My heart falls. I guess I'm going to keep being hungry. Nervously, I glance at the bowl of fresh fruit nearby and wonder how much it will take to feel satisfied till I can get to a market.

Ottavia smiles. "Breakfast is out. Sabrina will make eggs if you like. She should be back in a moment. And Kenzi, your *pane* isn't out yet. We were waiting for you to arrive. Sabrina will get it for you in a moment. We didn't forget you."

I'm so relieved. You have no idea how hard it is to find safe bread when you're outside of your house unless you've lived with this crap yourself.

Sabrina, who can't be a day out of high school, scoots into the kitchen, tying on her apron. She must have heard Ottavia because she grins at Lauren and me and immediately pulls a loaf of bread from a bag on the counter and slices off two pieces.

After breakfast, we finally get to see our room. It's as lovely as the rest of the villa. A huge canopy bed sits against the left wall. Maple head and footboard, carved with grapes and vines, stained a smoky brown. White translucent canopy. Creamy walls with paintings of flowers. Tall picture windows with white drapes that match the canopy. I could definitely stay here a while. At least a month.

I flop down on the bed. "Why did I need you to talk me into this? This place is amazing!"

Lauren joins me, and we both lay down. "Seriously. I can't believe that this is our lives right now."

I know. I'm glowing with happiness. And only the teeniest little voice in the back of my head is knock knock knocking and saying that I need to make sure that Christmas is taken care of. That everyone is depending on me.

It can kindly shut up. For now.

The shower feels glorious, and I'm thankful that my neck has loosened up without much effort on my part. I put on jeans, a long sleeve teal shirt, and my jacket and boots. Lauren and I return to the main floor and exit into the garden to explore a bit till we officially meet everyone at lunch and get started on the dig right after.

The lunch table is crowded with 18 people. And loud. But it's a good loud. I hear English and Italian, lots of excited people talking quickly. I actually talk a little with Alessia and Lena, who are to be our dig partners. They seem sweet. Sisters who decided this would be fun, just like Lauren and I did. They both have broad smiles that reach their almond brown eyes when they laugh, loads of long black hair, and a ready warmth that welcomes Lauren and I in. I think we'll be fast friends.

"I'm working on my PhD in archaeology with an emphasis on the late Roman Empire," Lena says. "My goal is to be a guest lecturer all over Europe so I can see everything. I don't get out of Italy much, especially since I started my doctorate."

"Have you started your dissertation?" I ask.

She nods. "It's on the reign of Domitian. He was awful. Very interesting. Our mother is friends with Ottavia, so that's how Alessia and I were invited. Alessia managed to get a sub for the last couple weeks of school. She's a third-grade teacher. From what Mama said, I think the dig area could be part of Domitian's estate, since there are prehistoric bones there. He was known to have a griffin skeleton."

"A griffin skeleton?" I'm intrigued.

"They assumed that it was a griffin because they didn't know it was actually other extinct animals' bones. I love this stuff." She sips her tea. "So, when ancient peoples found bones, they made up stories about them, invented creatures that they could have been."

"Oh right," I say. "They wanted to be able to explain everything in the world like seasons and the sun going across the sky."

"Yes," Lena continues. "So, it makes sense that they did the same with unique bones they found. Then the rich and famous were always claiming that they had the bones or bodies of these fantastic creatures. Emperor Claudius claimed to have a centaur, which was likely a trick where someone attached a horse and a human body. They kept it in honey to preserve it, so people had trouble telling that it was a fake. There were claims of satyrs too, half-human half-goat creatures. That would be another easy one to fake. But the bones. That always intrigues me. You usually find skeletons scattered because the soft tissue isn't around to hold them together properly anymore, so when ancient humans found them, they put them together however they thought they fit."[1]

I'm certain that I'm staring at her with my mouth agape. Is this where all the mythical creatures came from? It makes sense that people were trying to answer questions about the world around them and not just sitting around high from smoking whatever grew in the field behind their house, making up stories. The stories would have a purpose.

Lena continues. "What's fascinating is that ancient humans recognized that the bones they found didn't seem to come from any creatures they knew, so they assumed that they were from extinct creatures. Except the griffin. That's the strange one. They believed that griffins lived in the desert and guarded gold. It's pretty interesting if you think about it."

---

[1] Information about ancient peoples and their discovery and classification of fossils was gleaned from Adrienne Mayor's book *The First Fossil Hunters: Paleontology in Greek and Roman Times*. (Princeton University Press, 2000)

"That's fascinating." I say. My head is spinning now. This could be more interesting than I originally thought.

Gianmarco stands just then, so we stop talking. "Friends," he begins. In English, thank God. "I thank you for joining us here on our little adventure. First, a toast to you for coming." He raises his wine glass. "I realize that this is an unusual place for everyone to find themselves a few weeks before Christmas, and among strangers. But I hope that we will bond and end this journey as friends with an interesting story. I can't say what we will find, but may we find it in safety and good health. *Salute*."

"*Salute*." We all raise our glasses and drink. It's a Chianti, tasting of cherry, oak, and smoke. It's quite good.

Lunch nerves start as soon as we sit down, but I remember that Ottavia took care of me at breakfast and am pleasantly surprised that I actually get a plate of ricotta-filled ravioli, just like everyone else, but mine is gluten free. Huge sigh of relief! And it is delicious! The salad and grilled chicken are great too. Maybe I'll be OK here!

As we finish, Gianmarco stands again. "I want to give you a little background on the dig before we go outside. We started the excavation for an event venue for the estate but discovered huge bones and pottery. Then a little deeper, tile floor. That's when we contacted *Universitá di Studi Storici*—the University of Historical Studies in Rocca di Papa—to talk to them about the prudence of continuing our dig. They asked us to halt and sent *Professore* Salvatore Rossi," Gianmarco gestures to a gentleman in his early 30s in a light robin's egg blue sweater and jeans, "who specializes in artifacts of the Roman Empire, to oversee removal of whatever we find and determine if the area needs to be preserved as a historical site."

"So, it's definitely Roman Empire era?" Lena asks. Her eyes sparkle, and I can tell she's really excited about it.

"Based on the pottery shards that were sent to my office," Dr. Rossi, the professor on loan, begins, "we believe that the area was occupied around the first or second century AD."

"And what about the bones?" Lena asks.

"They are much older," the professor answers. "My assumption is that they were found in the area when the buildings were erected during the Roman Empire and then used for decoration or ceremonies."

Lena grins and leans toward me. "Domitian's griffin." She clasps her hands excitedly but soundlessly.

The professor appears to have heard her. "We aren't making any assumptions." He sounds stern, but he gives her a smile and a nod.

———

The dig area isn't terribly far from the house, so a short time after lunch, we all walk across the yard to it. A huge white tent envelops it, protecting it from the elements, and they have heaters, so it's in the high 60s in the tent, a bit warmer than the outside air. It's sunny today, so it won't be so bad, but with clouds or wind, it would be unpleasant.

After a short tutorial, Lauren, Alessia, Lena, and I are escorted to our dig area and given our tools.

"There's nothing more real than dirt," Lena says. She immediately squats and starts chipping away at the ground, slowly removing small chunks of earth with care. The rest of us emulate her.

Lena's words are spinning in my head. "Nothing more real than dirt." It's like all the stuff I was worried about—the new job with Divya Shanti, the Christmas dinner, figuring out how to be better, perfect, gah, I don't know—doesn't really matter. It's just me and the dirt. And someday, all the pieces that I have so worried about will be buried with time. Maybe it won't ever be important again.

Feeling my mortality right now. Creepy.

As my thoughts wander, I continue digging. Into the past. Into history. Who walked here before us? What did they leave? And I feel strangely calmer than I have in months.

Suddenly, my trowel makes a sharp sound that sets my teeth buzzing. "I think I found something."

Lena jumps up and brushes her hand against her olive chinos. "Can I see?"

I pick up a brush and work around where the clink happened. I see terracotta emerging.

"It's pottery. Work carefully around it with these," she hands me some smaller picks and chisels. "You don't want to damage it." She grins.

"I can't wait to see what you have there," Alessia says. Lauren nods excitedly and then bends back over her area with her trowel.

The minutes slip by as I continue to remove grain by grain of dirt ... maybe I'm exaggerating, but it seems like I'm barely making any progress. Finally, a four-inch chunk of a vase is sticking out of the earth. It has a design on it, but nothing that seems that special. Just some swirls. Maybe part of an arm? I can't tell.

How deep does this thing go? Maybe I should wiggle it a bit to loosen the dirt. In my head, this will work like extracting a tooth, but in reality ... I give it a little tug. I tip it back and forth. And then I hear a snapping sound that makes me want to puke.

I think I broke it. I broke a 2,000-year-old vase. That's a million years of bad luck, right? My face is burning, so I know I'm all red. And we've only been out here a few hours.

Suddenly, I hear my mom in my head. *"Kenzi! Be more careful. I can't believe you broke my grandmother's vase. You're always dancing where you're not supposed to!"* She was right. I was doing something I wasn't supposed to be doing and broke something important.

"You OK Kenzi?" Lauren says. She's sitting with her arms resting on her legs, her sleeves pulled up. She looks like she's really been working.

I was going for it. I thought I was doing it right. I just can't do this. I guess. I don't know.

"I'm taking a break," I say. The tears are welling in my eyes, and I don't want anyone to see. There is a table with artifacts nearby, so I slip the pottery shard onto it as I walk by and head to the spigot at the back of the house. I wash my hands and boots and leave them by the back door. The boots. Not my hands. Inside, my tennis shoes are waiting for me, along with over a dozen other pairs of shoes for the rest of the team to wear in the house. It honestly looks like a kid's birthday party at a bounce park with all the shoes there.

I head to the kitchen and make some tea for myself while I think about being a total failure. I had one job, and I already busted pottery on the first day of the dig.

I guess what Jennifer Halliday was saying in her book though is that I shouldn't be berating myself for a mistake because no one else is as concerned about it as I am. And that's probably true. But I am still beating my head against the wall, figuratively of course, because … could I be any clumsier? Why did I think I could pull that vase out? Am I like King Arthur or something? Ugh.

Maybe I'm just overwhelmed. I need to get out of my head.

"I thought you were in here beating yourself up." Lauren is standing in the doorway.

"I can't believe I chipped the pottery."

"Are you a professional archaeologist?"

"No."

"I bet they make mistakes too, you know."

Cori Wamsley

"I don't want to piss off *Professore* Rossi." I go heavy on the Italian accent and the rolled Rs.

"He seems like a decent human from the bit I heard at lunch. He probably won't crucify you. It wasn't like you broke something that wasn't already broken, you know."

"That's true. I just made it broken-er."

"And that happens." Lauren snags a piece of *pane* and smears plum jam on it. She takes a bite and makes a face like she has just slipped into a warm bath. After a minute, she turns to me. "Want to go back?"

Lauren commits a cardinal sin by eating her bread and walking in Italy, but no one but me saw her do it. We return to the dig, and Alessia and Lena are chugging water, also taking a break.

"There she is," Alessia says.

"I knew you'd be back," Lena adds. She gestures at the various piles of dirt that the team is working on. "There's history all around us. How can you not be seduced by it?"

Chapter 6

If I bit my nails, I likely would have nibbled them all the way off yesterday.

I'm still beating myself up for breaking that pottery ... If I could actually ruin ruins, I'm sure I would do that as well. No one seemed concerned. In fact, Alessia is brave enough to ask Dr. Rossi if artifacts sometimes get damaged, and he actually says that it happens all the time on these digs. That he doesn't expect amateurs to be perfect.

He said "amateurs" nicely, like he wasn't actually insulting us, but I'm sure that in his heart of hearts, he feels a little sad every time a piece of pottery gets dinged up. I mean, that's how people are with their passion, right?

I kinda wish she had asked him privately so he wouldn't have spoken in English to all of us as a group, again being kind.

Major guilt.

Luckily though, I pull myself together—Lauren threatened to kick my ass—and make it to the dig today.

This morning, we can smell the lemon trees again, and it is divine. There's almost a clean, spring-like feel to being outside here, and I love it. I dig it. Ha!

Maybe I won't screw up today. Geez.

As I'm leaning over a new chunk of dirt that looks like the other chunks of dirt that my team is examining, Lena mentions that she was doing some digging online last night in JSTOR—apparently a digital library of articles and books that graduate students use for their research—and she found something particularly interesting.

"So, I read in the article that Domitian's wife, Domitia, was rumored to have a lover who she would sneak off to see," Lena begins. "Of course, the Roman people agreed that this is why she and Domitian didn't have any heirs. The gods were punishing them."

I smile. It's amazing what we humans used to believe.

"The article said that there was no evidence of the affair, aside from, possibly, little trinkets of jewelry that the man gave her. She told Domitian they were family jewels from her parents whenever he found them." Lena brushes some dirt and peers closely at where she is digging before she continues.

"It's so sad that she had to sneak off," Lauren says. "I wonder if she was unhappy with Domitian or if she was in love before she had to marry him."

"She was married before and was made to leave her husband to marry Domitian," Lena explains.

"That really is sad," Alessia agrees. "I can't imagine leaving my husband to marry someone I didn't love, let alone really know."

"Romance was pretty different back then," I say. "Women were just pawns in a bigger game."

"You are right," Lena continues. "Domitia was traded from one husband to another. You know she didn't have any say. It was for the good of the country. For improving both families' security and aligning them with strong ties."

I barely heard her, though. I was thinking about something I said to Thomas …

… *"How does someone even do this?" I said. I was fuming. Just seeing him infuriated me. It was like putting my hand on a hot stove. There was no other way to react.*

And he didn't say a word. I could feel him staring at the wall calmly, like my existence didn't even faze him. What kind of person …

"I guess I'm nothing but a toy to you," I said.

Still nothing. He didn't deny it. Maybe some people never got away from seeing people as pawns in their game of life.

"Clearly we're done, Kenzi," Thomas finally said. "Why keep talking about it?"

He was so cool when he spoke. Like nothing I said could stir his soul. Does he even have one? ...

I frown and keep digging.

"Penny for your thoughts?" Lauren says.

I scowl forcibly at her till I realize she actually has a coin in her hand. "Are you seriously going to pay me? Because I have soooo many things on my mind. I actually think it's worth more than a penny."

"How about whatever Roman currency they used in Domitian's time?" Lauren grins.

She is right. It is seriously a very old coin, a little nicked up. You can clearly see a man's head on it though. He has a really thick neck and is wearing a wreath of laurel leaves. On the other side is a man on a horse. "This is amazing."

"Lena, is this one of Domitian's coins?" Lauren asks.

Lena seems impressed. "It is. I didn't think we would find something like that here. Usually, coins get snatched up pretty quickly."

As Lauren runs off to show Dr. Rossi her find, the rest of us return to digging. That one coin gives me hope that I'll find more pieces of the pottery that I found yesterday. And I start to wonder if maybe I could find all the pieces and start putting the vase together. Is that what they will do with it? Or will it always be just a handful of chunks that don't match up?

It kind of feels like a metaphor for my life.

How do all these things fit together? Do I stay in Pittsburgh? Run away? Do people run away to avoid big scary projects at work? Or the feeling of failure that comes with a nasty breakup? Or responsibility with your family? I mean, I did run away, but I have to go back. For now. But for how long? And won't it just be the same elsewhere?

How will I ever trust anyone again?

But if I don't miraculously get a job in another city this month, not that I'm looking, how can I pull off hosting Christmas? And make sure Declan's kids have all their stuff? And plan a flipping headquarters for Divya Shanti?

For real. *Divya Shanti*. She's going to find out that I have no idea what I'm doing. I have to make sure the whole thing goes off without a hitch, and I can't even dig up pottery!

What a nightmare that's going to be!

———

Tonight's dinner is possibly more delicious because we had been digging in the dirt the entire day.

As we meet in the dining room, we are greeted by spaghetti, savory grilled chicken, fresh salads, and bruschetta. It turns out that there is a huge garden behind the villa, and all the vegetables came from there. Crisp lettuce, ripe tomatoes, red onion, sliced black olives, Parmesan cheese, and pepperoncinis for a kick. I sip a glass of Sangiovese with my dinner, and it is like I had never tasted anything so wonderful before. I discover notes of leather, plum, and vanilla ... and probably some other things. I'm not great at picking out all the tastes in wine.

Maybe garlic? Do Italian wines taste like garlic? Maybe that was the bruschetta.

Just as I'm starting to think that the food is a great way to convince me to run away and live here permanently, I hear sharp voices coming from the foyer.

They are arguing. Probably in Italian. Because it's not English. And we're in Italy.

Still seated at the dining table, Ottavia looks concerned. Gianmarco looks angry. He jumps to his feet and stalks through the dining room. The front door slams before he gets there, and a sob reverberates through the house.

Because we have all fallen silent, I hear hushed voices hissing in the foyer, still in Italian, before Gianmarco returns.

"Raffaella?" Ottavia says under her breath. She purses her lips and shakes her head.

"*Si. E* Eduardo." Gianmarco jerks his chair out and sits forcefully. Slowly, chatter resumes at the table.

I raise my eyebrows at Lauren, but she just shrugs and takes a big gulp of her Sangiovese. "Do you taste leather?" she whispers.

"I thought so too."

After dinner, I need to get some shopping done for my nieces and nephews. Lauren had asked Annie, who apparently lives across the street from me back home—that's what Lauren said, since I've never met her—if I could ship packages to her, and she would hang onto them for me.

I pull up Onio on my phone. It's a new shopping app that my brother suggested a few months ago. They have literally everything under the sun, and I have an account with them, so free shipping. Yay!

Declan said that his daughter Lennox wants roller skates. And she said her favorite color is "flamingo." She told us that once when she was like four, and everyone laughed at how clever that was, so now she always says it. She's eight now, so it hasn't gotten old for her.

"Flamingo roller skates," I type into the search bar.

Holy moly. I found roller skates with flamingos on them. In her size.

But will she like them? Does she like actual flamingos? Or is this going to be one of those would-have-been-perfect presents if it was just the color and not the animal. Like how people like the color "salmon," but they probably don't want an actual salmon on their stuff.

Gah. How should I know? Maybe her sister Reese would be easier to shop for.

I mark the skates with a heart so I can come back to them later ... but not too much later because I don't want them to sell out. And I don't want to risk them not arriving in time.

I'll just check my email instead.

Yes, it's my work email. And I'm not supposed to be working. But I have a compulsion. Maybe this is *actually* why I have gray hair ...

The first email is from Miranda. It says to stop checking my email while I'm on vacation. Oh, she knows me too well. And she'll be able to see that I opened it too. Drat.

I skim through and see one from Logan.

> Hi Kenzi,
>
> I hope you're having fun! Find anything interesting yet?
>
> Here's my address if you have a chance to send a card. I'd love to see what you're seeing!
>
> Logan

I note his address in my contacts and jot off a reply.

> Hi Logan,
>
> We are having a great time! Lauren found a coin today from the early Roman Empire, which was really neat.
>
> I'll definitely send a postcard! This place is beautiful!
>
> Kenzi

Is that too short? I don't want to be rude. I don't want to gush and be weird though. It's probably OK. I need sleep.

Dig day three proves that this is nothing like what I imagined. Yes, we have an absolutely gorgeous view of the lake, and the sky is the most pristine blue I've ever seen. There has to be a gemstone this color. Maybe aquamarine. That doesn't even do it justice. And the smell of lemons is so pleasant. But as I look at yet another chunk of dirt in my hands ... I realize that this is just a lot of dirt. All day, just dirt. Honest dirt. No artifacts. At least not where I'm looking.

There's a team doing more painstaking work about 20 yards away. This is where the dig originated, where the excavators found the floor. It's a really interesting floor, but I have to wonder if what they are doing is actually any more interesting than what we're doing. You don't get that jolt of adrenaline when you think you've found something. Just brushing off this tile and that tile and chipping away a little more at the edge to find ... more tile.

I believe that Dr. Rossi said a mosaic stretches across the floor, but from where we are sitting, about eight feet above floor-level, a few yards away, it's hard to tell. I gaze across at it for a moment. A geometric pattern in mostly beige with charcoal, butterscotch, and brick red elements. A curl drifting around part of the design. I wonder if this space could be a dining room. Or a living room. Or maybe a bedroom. Who lived there? Or could it be a shop?

I sigh. I realize that not every day is going to be full of exciting finds. This isn't a game, and we aren't kids. No one went through and hid things for us to find.

It sort of feels like failure, though.

I wonder if Dr. Rossi expects us to keep finding things. Maybe he has an expectation for the haul. Maybe he has to find a certain number of items or the university will pull funding. Is that how this stuff works? Or are they cool with us just sifting through dirt and being like, "We found a lot of dirt today. Definitely some of the oldest dirt we've had the privilege of playing in." I chuckle at that thought.

It's only day three, and I'm already loopy. Lauren gives me a curious look and keeps digging.

I shower at the end of our shift and throw on some breezy black pants with comfy flats, a pink blouse, and a jacket. It's still sunny, and the air is perfect for a walk. I join Lauren, Lena, and Alessia heading into town for dinner, ready to brave the cultural barrier.

Maybe.

Lena and Lauren are chattering away about something they heard another team found. I think some clay beads. And I'm having a bit of a panic. I know enough Italian to find a bathroom or a library. Because that's really important when I can't read much Italian, right?

"Alessia," I hate asking this, "how do I tell the server that I can't have gluten?"

"Gluten?" Alessia looks confused.

"I have a food allergy to gluten, like in wheat. Can I tell the server so I don't get sick?"

"Oh. Yes," Alessia pats my arm. "It's OK. They are very good about that here. I imagine you thought that all they would have is pasta, no?"

"I did," I say. "Is that offensive?"

Alessia cackles. "Not at all. *Sono celiaca.*"

I murder the words repeating them. Probably not something I want to screw up. I get so frustrated and nervous and everything else when I have to tell people about my allergy. I know some people think it's a fad or I'm just on a weird diet to lose weight. I hate having to rely on someone else to keep me from getting sick, and that makes me feel so pathetic and desperate and agitated. It's no wonder I'm stumbling over the words.

After a couple tries, though, I'm good. Ready to tell people that pasta makes me sick. In the place where everyone eats pasta. Awesome.

I swallow hard so I don't break down in tears. I look at the group of women I'm with and think about how powerful we are together. They won't laugh. They will support me. They get me ... *right*?

We enter Il Piccolo Colibrì café on the main street, which looks cozy. It's fairly noisy with the dinner crowd, but we find a table.

"The name of the café means 'little hummingbird,'" Alessia says.

"That's sweet." I look around at all the people there and see why. Chatting amicably with their tablemates, everyone seems to be enjoying themselves. Children and servers flit around the café. The tightly packed tables make the room feel more closed in than it is. Stone walls stretch to the ceiling, which is covered in tin tiles from long ago.

We order *panini*. Mine is a *panino*—that's a single *panini*—*con porchetta*, which is pork, and I add cheese and tomatoes. I say "*Sono celiaca*," and the server seems to know what to do. Alessia says a few things to her, and she nods.

"They have gluten-free bread for you," Alessia says. Thank goodness!

"Isn't the woman in the blue sweater part of our group?" Lauren asks. A couple tables over, a lady with blonde hair streaked with gray is wearing sunglasses and enjoying a *panino*. She has a sky-blue sweater with a wide knit, and a white cane rests against her chair.

"She's by herself," Lena says. "Should we invite her to join us?"

I have a mini-panic attack because we don't want to say the wrong thing and offend her. She's here alone, so maybe she wants to be alone. Or maybe she's lonely and wants us to ask. But she's already halfway through her meal, and we just ordered. So, she would have to sit there and watch us eat. Rather, not *watch*, since I'm assuming she's blind: the cane.

Lauren snickers, and I realize she's watching me as I play out all the scenarios in my head. "If we don't ask her, then we won't give her the chance to do what's best for her, which could be a yes *or* a no."

"Good point," I say.

Lena hops up, and we hear her speaking to the woman, who turns to face her and appears to be listening intently. Then Lena beckons to a passing server. "*Scusi.* Could we add Julie to our group?"

Soon, Julie, the woman in the blue sweater, is seated at our table as well, and we are all introducing ourselves.

"Everyone in the dig group is so friendly," she says with a beautiful British accent. "One of my teammates offered to order a rideshare for me, but Hugo, my nephew, walked with me. He's picking up some souvenirs, so I am enjoying some local cuisine. I love getting out and exploring, but it's obviously a little tough in new places." She taps her glasses. "Thank goodness his semester wrapped up in time to come with me."

"Understandable," Lauren says. "What made you want to come do the dig?"

"I want to fall in love," Julie says. Then she laughs. "Really. I want to fall in love with new places. I just adore them. Before I lost my sight, I traveled a lot for my work, so I'm used to it. I went to Bangkok, Negril, Cairo, Seattle, Copenhagen … all over. Then boom. I was blind as a bat and had to stay home. It was dreadful."

"How did you get the courage to travel again?" I ask.

"Stonehenge."

"The circle of standing stones?" Alessia says.

"Yes," Julie continued. "A dear friend told me, 'Enough moping around, Jules. Out of the house with you.' And we drove to Stonehenge. It had been so long since I went somewhere new. I thought that the only way to experience a place was with my eyes. Was I naïve!"

I feel like time has stopped for a moment. Have I been seeing and feeling and breathing while I'm here in Italy? Am I limiting myself?

"When I got out of the car," Julie said, "I heard so much. The grass whispering, the little bugs flitting around. A couple of other tourists talking softly across the circle. But I could *feel* too. I knew which direction the stones were in because I could *feel* their immenseness. And there was the slightest vibration beneath my feet. I never gave myself the chance to feel it before. But there it was. That's when I realized that places are more than a pretty postcard to put in your keepsake. They are to be experienced; they are everything."

I want that, I thought. I want to go somewhere and feel something. I want the ground to quiver and really let me know that this is a place I am experiencing.

Unless it's an earthquake.

Chapter 7

On day four, I find a bead.

And I don't break it. Or chip it. Or drop it. Or lose it.

I place it on the table with the other artifacts, and Dr. Rossi no longer hates me and thinks I'm incompetent.

At least, he thanks me and says it is wonderful. He seems excited about the bead. And I'm guessing he had a previous opinion because I broke the pottery before. Not that he knew. Maybe I'm projecting.

The bead is pretty cool. Not remarkable. A lot like the other beads that were found in the area. Blue and brown glass barrels. Thick and bulky. Clearly a statement piece of jewelry.

Lena comes with me to drop it off, and she stays to chat with Dr. Rossi about it. She's pretty excited too, which is sort of funny. She's excited about *everything* we find.

As I watch them talking, I realize that they really seem to get each other, which is so nice. It's wonderful when you talk with a colleague and both love what you do. They both have a twinkle in their eyes, and their voices are getting louder. Lena's hand gestures are getting wilder.

I hope she doesn't knock stuff off the table.

I turn back to the dirt. *The just dirt.* I dig. Sometimes it's soothing. Sometimes I don't even notice what I'm doing because my brain is a million miles away going over all the conversations I've had where I should have said something different. More empowered. Or witty. Whatever.

But my trowel chinks on something again, and I proceed with the smaller tools: a pick, a brush. Gently wiping away millennia of dirt and pollen and whatever else was in the world. Poop? Probably. Ew.

When I finally clear the ... dirt, I realize that it's another bead, identical to what I found before. Now I'm excited! I put the bead in my jeans pocket and dig around for another 30 minutes hoping to find more, but there's nothing.

Reluctantly, I stand, pull the solo bead from my pocket, and head back toward the tables with the artifacts.

"Did you find something else?" Lena leaps from her spot and chases after me.

I show her the bead and explain that I found two but no others.

She smiles. "Dr. Rossi and I were talking about the first bead you found. It matches the description of a necklace that Domitia wore that was named in one of Pliny the Younger's epistles. It turns out that we read the same article about the necklace. According to the author, the necklace was assumed by Pliny to be a gift that Domitia claimed was an heirloom. But there was no record of her family owning it. Did you know that Domitian banished all philosophers from Italy during his reign? He didn't like it when they criticized him."

"I didn't know that."

"Dr. Rossi and I have the same hunch, that there was a house here where Domitia and her lover met. It's close enough that it would be convenient for her to sneak away from the palace but also far enough away that no one would suspect it if they saw her out walking toward the lake."

"That's fascinating," I say. I'm curious about the necklace now. "But the necklace is broken."

"It's hard to tell if it was broken before it was buried or as the ground shifted," Lena says, "but I'm betting that it was before. If it happened after, then we would likely find more beads in the immediate area."

"Good point."

"So, my next question is *why was it broken before?* Did Domitian suspect that his wife was receiving gifts from another man?"

I close my eyes for a moment and picture Domitia wearing the necklace, happy, dreamy even. And then her husband approaches, sees that look, knows but can't prove anything. He snatches her necklace and rips it from her neck, like that scene in *Cinderella* where the stepsisters reclaim the stuff that they threw out earlier because they don't want Cinderella to wear it. She falls to the floor sobbing as beads go everywhere. And mice scurry around trying to gather them—

Maybe not.

Funny how that wisp of happiness can so easily be destroyed ...

"Kenzi? Are you OK?" Lena touches my arm.

"Just ... imagining."

"Mmm, I do the same thing when I see this stuff. It's more than just 'What was life like?' It's 'What was their story?'"

———

After that, we don't find anything for a couple days, so the dig site is pretty quiet. We chat a bit, but the overall mood is peaceful. Which is funny to me because I thought we would all be sad when we weren't actively finding things. Sure, my mood went up and down a bit at first, relying on those dopamine hits from finding stuff, but I think I got used to it. And it's just nice being out here. Calm. Just the smell of dirt and lemons and whatever local flowers and grasses are nearby. I didn't think dirt would smell nice, but the earthy smell is welcoming. Familiar at this point. Sure, I usually smell the dirt when I'm on-site checking a build for work, but this is different. It's historic dirt. I know that doesn't make sense. It's deep. Ha!

On the evening of the sixth day, we finish dinner and walk to the beach. It's a small group: Lauren and me, Lena and Alessia, Julie, a couple women from Julie's team, and Raffaella Zangari—Ottavia and Gianmarco's daughter. When she found out that we wanted to walk to the beach, Raffaella was excited to be our tour guide, and she insisted we call her "Ella."

Julie says something, and Ella laughs. She's leading the group, wearing a bronze trench over a green sweater and straight-legged pants with smart booties. Her dark glossy hair falls to mid-back, and her eyes betray the feelings behind her smile. Clearly, something is bothering her. Poor girl.

When we get to the beach, it's completely different from what I imagined. The sun is setting behind us, and the deeper blues and purples of the sky are reflected in the peaceful water in tones of tanzanite. Several bonfire sites are set up in an arc around the shore, and parties are already at some of them. Ella leads us to one that isn't occupied, and we spread out blankets and get out our picnic snacks while Lena and Alessia work on lighting the pile of branches.

A group of men at another bonfire waves at us, and Lauren walks over to say "hi." I recognize them from the group digging up the floor of the house. They look like they are being friendly to Lauren, but I can't get up the nerve to walk over and talk. I'll hang with the sorority for now.

When Lauren comes back, she sits down beside me and smiles. "They seem nice. Angelo, Dario ... I can't remember all their names." She laughs. "Angelo is the cute one. Three of them are brothers, and the other is a cousin. They all live in Italy, but I don't recall which cities. They told me a lot."

I try to casually look over and assess who the "cute one" is. "Describe the cute one?"

"Orange shirt, muscular, pretty eyes with thick lashes, though you can't see them from here."

"I think his most outstanding feature is his eyebrows. They even show up the orange shirt." They look like that Wooly Willy toy Declan and I had as kids with the face and the little magnetic chips that you move around to give him hair or eyebrows or a mustache and beard. Declan liked to keep him bald and give him giant eyebrows and facial hair.

Lauren smacks my arm playfully. "Come on. He's cute."

"If you like furries."

Lauren gags and scoops a handful of bread, cheese, and meat onto a plate.

"*Coppiette*" Ella says, as she points at one of the salted meats.

I nod and then grab a piece, along with some Parmesan, prosciutto, and fig jam. I pop a chunk of Parmesan in my mouth. Oh my God, it's so good!

I return to earth to discover that everyone else has bread, and I forgot to pack my stuff. I guess I can scoop up the jam with the ... ham? It rhymes! What did she call it? Boo. I hate feeling left out. I also realize that Ella is talking about the argument we overheard the other night.

"And I know everyone heard it. I'm so used to us arguing and completely forgot that we had guests. I was just so mad."

"Why do you guys argue so much?" Lauren says.

"Oh, this and that," Ella flicks her hand in the air. "He wants us to take a class at the same time. Well, it doesn't fit in my schedule. Or he wants to go to Rome for the weekend. Well, I had a test I was studying for. Or he wants to know who I was talking to at work. And it's none of his business. I talk to everyone at the restaurant. People who work there. People who come in. People who walk by and say hi when I'm cleaning up." Her voice gets higher, and she starts wringing her hands. "I'm a person, and I talk to other people. It means nothing."

Clearly that last one is a big problem.

"How odd that he doesn't like that." Everyone else was quiet, and I wasn't sure what to say. So, I say that. Does that help? Am I supposed to make her feel better?

"Well! He's always accusing me of talking to Gino, who I work with and have to talk to, and then he's upset because I have Gino's phone number. *In case I need someone to cover my shift. It happens.*" At this point, she's fuming. "And the other night, he said that I'm probably *kissing Gino behind his back* and laughing about it. I love Edo. I would never do that!"

"That's awful," I agree.

"What does he say when you talk to him about this?" Lauren asks.

"He says that he wouldn't be concerned if I wasn't always cheating on him. I have *never* cheated on him. We've been together for three years and not even once. I never even thought about it. He's my soulmate."

Sounds more like a cellmate ...

"I wonder why he's so hung up on this," Lauren says.

"It's very odd that he would keep accusing you of cheating, Ella," Lena says. "Did his last girlfriend cheat on him?"

"He was 15, so it was all very innocent. She still lives here in town. I think she's engaged to someone, last I heard." Ella sighs. "And I want us to be happy. I want us to get married once we finish university. We only have two more years. He says I'm definitely not ready to be serious or for marriage *as much as I cheat on him*, and it makes me so angry to always be accused for no reason."

I'm just shaking my head in disbelief because this story is utterly insane. But then, I remember what college was like and all the odd beliefs we had about life. Heck, I'm not one to talk after what happened with *my* last boyfriend.

"Men can be something else," Lauren says. I think she's trying to calm Ella down and shift the weight of the conversation. "Sometime, Kenzi and I need to tell you guys a story. It's pretty nuts."

"That's a story for another night. I'm enjoying this cheese too much." I take a bite of pecorino Romano and fig jam. I grin and close my eyes in glee.

"I need some of that immediately." Ella grabs some mozzarella and sundried tomatoes and breathes out heavily.

———

My head is reeling from Ella's story when Lauren and I get back to the room.

"I know what you're thinking," Lauren says, "but our story definitely tops Ella's."

I raise my eyebrows. "I'm not ready to share that yet. It's still pretty raw."

"You don't mean that."

"OK, it's embarrassing."

"That's more like it. And it's not embarrassing. You had no idea what he was doing. It's not like there was a sign or anything."

"I know."

"I'm not forcing you to talk about it. I just think it would have helped Ella to know that there are other crazy relationships out there."

"I don't want to normalize it!"

Lauren sighs. "I know."

We both turn to our phones, and I check my email. Compulsively. I actually forgot that I wasn't supposed to. Bad Kenzi.

There's an email from Logan, which just says, "How's the pasta?" I know, I'm in Italy, ha ha. It is nice of him to ask though. So I reply that I had amazing mushroom risotto at dinner last night, which has honestly been on my mind off and on today because sometimes I don't get that lucky with gluten-free food.

"Are you checking your email?"

"Aren't you?"

"I'm actually playing mahjong."

"Oh."

"So, you are?"

"I forgot I wasn't supposed to."

"So, it's work email."

"Yeah ..."

"Kenzi! You are on vacation. And you deserve a break."

"I was just telling Logan about dinner."

"I see ..."

"What?"

"Nothing." Lauren smirks.

"I work with him. He asked. I'm being nice."

"Were you hoping to see an email from Logan and that's why you opened your work email?"

"You are infuriating." I close my phone and hop off the bed. "I'm going to read that book."

"I love how you call it 'that book' like it's Voldemort."

I pick up "that book" and grin. "I'm about to read *Trusting Your Superpowers* by Jennifer Halliday. It got five stars on Amazon, over 300 reviews, and has a top 100 ranking in the Women's Personal Growth category. One reader said *Halliday is a total genius for hacking our superpowers! I can't imagine how I would have jumped into that burning jet and saved that puppy while the jet was flying if I hadn't read this book! Jennifer Halliday for president!*

"I'll give you ten dollars if you actually post that as your review when you're done."

I snort-laugh and get out my journal. I have some serious reading to do if I'm going to find any superpowers and get my head on straight when I get back. A nervous tremor ripples through my stomach. We've already been here a week, two left. I somehow managed to forget all the looming stress that will be mine again when I return home.

Divya freaking Shanti. Headquarters. And Christmas with the fam, of course. I put the book down. How am I going to handle all that? I have to make everyone happy!

"Put your nose back in that book, Kenz," Lauren says. "I know that face. Be present. Stressing now won't make things better in the future but reading that book will."

"I hate it when you're right." I begin chapter five and start taking notes on my feelings and my superpowers.

Chapter 8

I spent breakfast drooling over some of the neighboring villas as I walked the grounds, munching on cornetto *senza glutine* with speck—cured meat—and mascarpone cheese. After that, I am dying to know how they plan to create a building that works with everything surrounding it. And what the whole thing would look like. And I kinda miss drawing and working on buildings, so yes, I am being a nerd.

I spot Gianmarco sitting outside, enjoying a cup of espresso, so I walk over. "What are you planning for the event center? ... once the dig is over, of course," I ask.

He laughs. "Lauren said you would probably want to go over blueprints with me."

"I don't mean to be nosy," I rush. Maybe I shouldn't have said anything. "I just wondered what it would look like and how it would fit in here. There are so many beautiful villas, and of course the natural beauty of the area, it's just ... maybe I'll have to come back and see it when it's done."

"That could be a while because of the dig. And I understand your curiosity." Gianmarco sips his drink. "It will be a two-story building with stucco that matches the villa. We plan on ample parking surrounding the building, along with beautiful gardens interwoven throughout the area. We want it to maintain the charm of our land and not be an overwhelming piece of concrete."

"I love that." I really do. I'm impressed by how much the indoor and outdoor work together here, almost speaking to each other, encouraging you to explore one and then the other and then return to where you started. I turn toward the dig site. "Are you planning to face the lake?"

"We are. It's such a lovely way to welcome visitors."

"Oh, I agree. You may want to do some large windows in the front to let in the morning sun, fewer in the back. It will also help having natural daylight to present your products like they would be seen on the street."

"Excellent point. We hadn't thought of that. I will have to speak to our architect about it." Gianmarco grins. "I'm glad I talked to you."

"Me too." I realize then that the stream of diggers from the villa had trickled to, well, just me. "I should probably catch up. Lots of random beads and chunks of pottery to hunt for!"

Gianmarco chuckles. "Absolutely. We really appreciate the work the volunteers have done. I must be getting to the workshop now. Ciao."

"It must smell heavenly in there!" I say. I mean, who doesn't want to smell leather all day. Ahhh.

Pausing, Gianmarco turns to look back at me. "It really does. Maybe I will offer a tour to the volunteers this week. It would be nice for you all to see what we are about."

"Count me in!" Touring a leather workshop? How cool is that!? And that's when it hits me that I'm truly an adult. It wasn't when I realized I have a favorite burner on my stove. It was being excited about a leather workshop tour. Oy.

As I walk toward the dig site, I realize that I didn't hold back on the window thing. I didn't go overboard and start redesigning the building for him. I just made the suggestion. And he appreciated it. It's not something he thought of. Of course it isn't! That's something I trained for. So, maybe, I can do this? Maybe? Divya Shanti's building is going to be another animal altogether, but if I can just speak to them like they are normal people and I'm a professional who knows exactly what I'm—

And that's when I catch my shoe on a root sticking out of the ground and nearly take a header into the artifacts tent.

No one saw that.

I walk around sites like this all the time. I should totally know to watch where I'm walking. Where is my head?

Oh, I was thinking about how I'm becoming more confident. Clearly.

I reach my group and greet them. They are already digging. The sun is shining brightly outside the tent, and the heaters are on inside. It feels like a spring day. I peel off my jacket and push up the sleeves of my taupe sweatshirt. Squatting in the dirt, I begin to dig. The group is a bit quiet today, but it's a good quiet. Honestly, the whole camp seems calm and happy, just poking away at the dirt with our various tools.

I hear a gasp of excitement from the group in the tile area, so I peer in their direction. It looks like they are uncovering more of that mosaic. I definitely need to check it out. I can hear them speaking rapidly in Italian, and one word jumps out at me: *pesce*. Fish! There is a fish on the mosaic. Cool!

I feel myself smiling and get a flutter of joy. It feels like the whole camp is humming now, even though there is only the excited chatter from the mosaic diggers. Fish. Something real. They ate that. They saw that. They thought it was worth decorating this house in fish. Not exactly my taste, but I get it. Another flutter of joy swims through me like goldfish fins. This is real, right here.

But we are still curious whose house this was. What happened with the beaded necklace? Did this house belong to a fisherman? Did people fish in this lake? Did you need to be a fisherman to have fish decorating your house? Wouldn't your wife kind of roll her eyes if you were THAT into your job?

Was Domitian into fish?

"What are you thinking about, Kenzi?" Lauren asks.

"Just wondering if Domitian liked fish," I say. Because that's totally normal.

"I still wonder about the griffin he supposedly had."

"He did have a griffin," Lena says. "There are articles about it. It was documented by several philosophers of the time."

"Right but, we know that all the churches in Rome had 'relics,'" I use air quotes here, "from dead saints that they used to get money from people. Visitors would pay to see the relics. How do we know that the supposed griffin wasn't something that they knew wasn't a griffin? If that makes sense.

We know that it wasn't a griffin, but did anyone from that time know?"

"I see what you mean. That's an interesting question. I don't know how we would find out about who knew the griffin was a fake." Lena pauses and looks like she is thinking. "I'm curious, though, if we can find information about Domitia's boyfriend. I looked for information before, but maybe now, if we approach this particular dig site as a potential spot where they were meeting up, we might be able to figure out what was here. And who was here."

While we were talking, the sun hid behind some clouds. For a while, we had breaks of sun and darkness, and now it's getting really dark.

"It smells like rain," Alessia says. She's brushing dirt away from what looks like yet another blue and brown bead. So gently. A brush and then a stare. Another brush and another stare. It's like she wants to see if it matches what the whole looks like in her mind. After a few more minutes, she plucks the bead from the ground. A piece of leather cord hangs from it. It's brittle and sticks out at a strange angle, bent in places. "Looks like another part of that necklace."

The sound of rain pelting the tent shakes us all from our activities. Gusts flap the edges of the tent, spraying those closest to the edge.

"Let's head in," Dr. Rossi calls. He pulls his bottle green jacket close around him and throws the hood over his wavy hair. After flicking off the heater, he stands by the tent "door" and ushers us all close so we can move as a pack back to the house. "It looks like we will be stuck inside a while. Corsica got it earlier, and it's still raining there. We were hoping it would blow south of us, but no such luck."

As I dodge out of the tent, I throw up the hood of my vibrant indigo jacket and jog through the lemon trees to the house. We are getting soaked. But there is no way around it. Lauren's jacket has changed from olive to deep green because it's soppy wet by the time we reach the house. She squeezes her braid in the mud room and laughs at the water that springs forth. I see that "cute" guy catch her eye and shake his head with mirth.

All 16 of us crowd around now, not sure what to do. I can see Dr. Rossi fighting an umbrella as he runs to his car. The wind and rain might keep us in for a while.

"Towels?" Sabrina has suddenly appeared with a huge stack of white towels that are about to become brown. And we all dry off. I feel a little guilty just leaving the towels in a pile, but that's what she says we should do. At least we aren't soaked as we slip back into our clean shoes and head to our rooms.

I think I hear Ella, so I turn when I get to the stairs. She's chatting with Nico as he and Sabrina gather towels. Ella is clearly talking passionately as her hands are gesturing in the air. And then I realize that Nico has completely stopped gathering towels and is looking at her like nothing else matters. Sabrina must have realized it too because she shuffles off to leave the two of them alone.

"Kenz, are you coming?"

I smile and continue up the stairs without a word.

"I think Nico likes Ella." We are finally in our room with the door shut, and both Lauren and I are pulling out clean clothes. My jeans have had it. There is mud splashed up to mid-thigh, so I'll have to do some laundry. I imagine everyone here is thinking the same thing.

"Wow, what makes you say that?" Lauren is slinking gently toward the bathroom door like she doesn't think I'll notice. I mean, we both know that there will be a fight for the tub. That's OK. I'll go second and just take longer.

I brief her on what I saw downstairs, and she smiles too. "Maybe she will figure it out." Then she calls, "Dibs!" and shuts the bathroom door behind her. I hear the tub running a minute later, so I peel off my jeans and shirt and wrap up in one of the fluffy white robes hanging in our closet. Oh my goodness! I feel like an empress. Or a rich Hollywood actress. Or a famous heiress. Anyway, it's amazing how a fancy robe can make you feel.

Of course, I compulsively check my phone and see an email from Logan. He's talking about how much he loves lasagna and that he's always wanted to try real Italian lasagna. That's cute. I'll answer in a minute.

I also have a text message from Mom. She's suggesting that I have a sweet potato dish because you "have to have a sweet potato dish" and I guess she's right. I never really paid attention to the "have to haves" at any other Christmas because they were just there for me to decide if I wanted to eat them or not. And now I like "have to have" sweet potatoes. But, I don't want to do the kind that always have the brown sugar and ... is it marshmallows? Do they always have marshmallows? Is that something else that I'm thinking about and getting them confused? What does that awful green bean one have in it ... oh, that's mushroom soup. Would marshmallows even work with green beans?

I'll just respond. *Sounds good! If you have a recipe you like, please email it to me, and I'll make sure it happens!* I want Mom to be happy. I want *everyone* to be happy, but especially Mom. And I want her to see that I can do this because—

There's a knock at the door. Is it inappropriate in Italy to open the door in my bathrobe? I'm covered. And I decide that I don't really care. I'm not putting those pants back on.

I answer it. "Hi, Sabrina!"

"Ciao, Kenzi. Gianmarco would like to invite you and Lauren to join the group after lunch for a tour of the leather workshop. He is securing cars to bring everyone over. Would you like to join them?" She's holding a clipboard and waiting for an answer.

"Definitely! And Lauren will come too. She's in the shower right now."

"Perfect. Please join the group in the foyer after lunch."

———

We enjoy a lunch of minestrone soup—they kept the pasta separate so I could enjoy it too!—sandwiches, and salad as the rain beats heavily on the windows.

Even the rain is beautiful here. The lake reflects a turbulent sky in grays and blues, the surface shattered by the storm. Nearby trees and bushes shimmy from the water smacking into them. Flowers bob their heads up and down. There is no end in sight.

We learn from Ella, who joins us for our meal, that the leather workshop is only ten minutes away, toward town. Gianmarco has cars waiting for us out front. It seems that everyone is excited to go, as the entire group of 16 is waiting in the foyer immediately after our meal for Gianmarco's instruction.

"Please join your dig group and get in the cars," Gianmarco says. "I will meet you at Pelletteria Zangari." He climbs into his sleek black sedan, and Ella joins him in the passenger seat.

We duck into a black Lincoln town car with Lena and Alessia, and I realize too late that Nico the same driver who picked us up at the airport, is driving. Lena is apparently ready to take one for the team and hops naively into the front seat. "Is it too late to run back in and make my will?" I hiss at Lauren.

She raises her eyebrows and smirks at me. "You'll be fine."

In my head, I ask every archangel and saint I can think of to protect us as we take the short trip to the leatherworks. This is Italy, so I imagine they can all hear me, what with Vatican City being here. Can't be too safe!

"The Pope has a vacation home in Castel Gandolfo, so if he's there right now, he might be able to hear you." Lauren says. She knows what I'm doing.

We dodge around a slower-moving car—yes in the pouring rain—and as my life flashes before my eyes, I drag my thoughts to the superpowers book I've been reading, trying to recall what Jennifer Halliday suggests we do when facing our fears, since that's the closest topic to "imminent death" that she covers. The chapter I read last night was called "Own It" because she uses it as a cutesy acronym for conquering anything. "Anything," she says, which I find hard to believe because there are things out there a little scarier than just calling for pizza or telling someone you like them. What about scorpions or bears or tsunamis ... maybe she just meant normal fears, but she really should have been more specific.

I tear my eyes away from the road as Nico takes a super sharp left, cutting across in front of the most gigantic truck ever. "OWN IT" somehow comes flooding back, and I desperately grab at it.

"Open your mind.

"Wwwwwww ... What the heck was "W" for?

"Name the fear.

"Invite the challenge.

"Take charge of what you desire."

"What are you talking about?" Lauren says. She's giving me a funny look, but we are bouncing all over the place on a cobblestone road, and my stomach is churning now, so I'm not that focused on what the look says.

"It's from the superpower book."

"Really?!" Now I see that she's thrilled. "You like it then?"

"Just searching for a healthy distraction." As I finish the sentence, Nico pulls up in front of a huge stucco building, right behind the other cars from the Zangari villa.

"When you finish this one, you should read Halliday's first book, *Famous in my Head*," Lauren says.

"You're joking."

"I read that last year," Alessia says. "It was so good for getting me into the right mindset to ask about an open position in third grade, where I felt more comfortable. I'm so glad I did, too. I love that age group!"

"So, you're saying that books like this really work?" I thought maybe it was just Miranda and

Lauren who read this stuff, but apparently others did it too.

"I absolutely believe in the power of books to change who we are," Lauren says. "It's been a game-changer since ... the incident last year."

I shake my head. "Not doing this." Then I hop out of the car and follow the rest of the group inside the workshop.

"On the left side of the workshop, through that door, is the tannery," Gianmarco explains. "This is where we cure, cut, dehair, *et cetera* to prepare the skins for tanning. It is also where we perform the actual tanning." He guides them through the door and down a hall to a room full of big rotating drums. "These are filled with our special recipe of water and tannins."

I know that word! It's like in red wine. The bitter part that makes your tongue feel like it's wearing a jacket.

"The recipes for tanning are different for each leather maker and have been kept a secret, in many instances, for centuries. Our process was actually perfected in the 1600s and has been passed down through the family."

He guides us to another room that looks very similar and explains that this is where the leather is dyed. In the next room, several men wipe hides with oils and waxes, which brighten the color immediately.

Soon, we are escorted across the main hall to the other half of the workshop, where they actually cut and stitch the leather products. And it smells heavenly!

I feel a hand clutch my shoulder and gasp. Lauren is making the shhhh face and motioning for me to jog off down a hallway with her. But the leather ...

I turn back toward the tour group, and Lauren grabs my arm again.

"Just come on," she hisses.

We take a few quiet steps toward the other end of the hall. It appears to open into a brightly lit room at the back of the building. I see a row of windows letting in tons of natural light, despite the dark storm clouds outside. Then I hear it: the hushed tones of a man and woman speaking ... in Italian. Damnit.

We peer around the corner and see Nico and Ella chatting. He's gazing at her in a way that speaks volumes, even if I don't know what the words are. And she looks like she's enjoying herself but is totally clueless that he has feelings for her. It's sort of adorable.

"I think he does like her," Lauren mouths as she agrees with my earlier assessment.

I need to tell Ella what I saw when Nico was cleaning up this morning. I'm no fan of his driving, but he seems like a decent guy. I give a thumbs up and mouth, "We should go," because I seriously don't want to get yelled at in Italian for snooping around in a leather factory. Or arrested. In Italian. I would be so confused.

My head is swirling now with the look on Nico's face, the smell of leather, and the idea of possibly being arrested—in Italian—and I just want to get back to the safety of the tour group ... when I hear heavy footsteps coming toward us. Noooo.

A conference room door on our left is open, so I duck inside, and Lauren follows.

"What are we—" Lauren whispers.

I cut off a symphony with my hands and flatten myself against the wall like I'm a shadow. Lauren eyes me and does the same. I can feel my heart in my throat.

If we get caught, I can always say we were looking for a bathroom. That's what they usually do.

"They" like the people in movies who get caught doing stupid things.

In Italian.

"Ah, Ella!" A jovial voice echoes down the hall. I think it's Gianmarco. And then Ella's lilt in reply. I hear Nico say something too, and they all laugh.

"Let's go," Lauren says. But I don't know. What if they come back this way?

We zip back to the foyer and peek into the leatherworking part of the building. The guard at the door must recognize us because he immediately opens it to let us in. I casually make use of the tiny bit of Italian that I do know, "*Lo siento. Bagno,*" except I think I said, "I'm sorry," in Spanish. But he doesn't seem to care.

Ahead, I see our group surrounding a gentleman who is running leather through a sewing machine, and we join them to watch. Zip, zip, zip. And he has the arm of a coat.

"Would anyone like to try?" the man asks. He looks like my grandfather and smiles like a teenager. He clearly loves his work.

"I would definitely sew my fingers together," I tell Lauren.

"You certainly would." Lauren purses her lips for a moment and then calls, "Me!" She pushes up through the group, and the man shakes her hand heartily.

"Come, you will make a purse." He picks up a sheet of forest green leather. "To match your eyes."

Lauren smiles and takes the leather like a pro. The man instructs her on how to hold it, but she clearly knows what she's doing. After a couple zips, she creates a little pocket. He pulls out a strap, which she also zips onto the pocket.

"Brava to our seamstress! Such beautiful handiwork. We could hire you, you know?"

"I'm actually a wedding dress designer back home," Lauren states.

How does she do that? She is so confident, but she doesn't sound cocky at all. Not that I have the chance to really tell people what I do, but still. I don't think I would have stepped up, especially if I'm that skilled. Does anyone think she's showing off? I *know* she's not. She's extremely talented. But still.

"Then we are lucky to have you demonstrate. I will have a snap affixed, and you can take this home with you." The man hands the purse off to a younger man, who rushes to a different part of the leatherworks.

Lauren pauses on her way back to me to chat with the heavily eyebrowed gentleman she spoke with the other night. Alfredo? Umberto? He says something and gestures toward the machine. Lauren gives a flirty laugh and says something cute in response, which makes him laugh too.

"She did a nice job," a woman's voice came from behind me.

I turned to see Ella. "She did. She's so talented."

"She did my sister's wedding dresses. I am hoping she will do mine soon as well ..."

"Do you think Edoardo will propose soon?" My stomach turns at the thought, after hearing about their arguments. Does she really think it's a good idea?

Ella scoffs. "I'm sure he will just keep telling me, 'I'm not ready.'"

"I'm sorry. It's tough when you have a dream and don't seem to get any closer to it." I massage the blank space on my left ring finger with my other hand and try not to feel the gush of emotions it brings.

"What dream have you lost, Kenzi?"

"It's a long story." And I'm nowhere near brave enough to venture into that territory again. At least not for a bit longer. "I'm reading a book right now, *Trusting Your Superpowers*, where the author talks about how dreams change as we grow, and it's OK. But sometimes, it's hard to believe that it's OK." I point at the bag in her hand, changing the subject. "Did you get something new?"

"I did." A devilish smile breaks across her face as she pulls a pair of ruby red leather flats from her bag. Oh envy! They are gorge! "Papa made these for me. He sometimes gives us little treats."

"Those are fabulous. You're one lucky lady!"

"Nico was saying that they are his favorite color. They are certainly beautiful." Her face grew cloudy again. "I was only talking to Nico. We have known each other a long time. We're just friends." Her clipped tone was protective.

"Ella, you don't have to explain. You can be friends with men. It's OK."

———

Domitia stepped out of her comfort zone. I can step out of mine. I know that's a bizarre thought, but I can't help putting the two together. On day eight, the rain drops back to a trickle, but yesterday's wind was so gusty that everything inside the tent got soaked. Dr. Rossi and his team set up fans this morning to dry it out. I doubt we will be back in till tomorrow.

Lena, Alessia, Lauren, and I retreat with a few others to the nerdery, I mean the library, which is in town, not a long walk from the villa.

Last night's reading from *Trusting Your Superpowers* was all about getting uncomfortable, which is a great topic if you like that icky feeling in your stomach that you're doing something you shouldn't be doing. Of course, the "uncomfortable" stuff is supposed to be a stretch like talking to a stranger or learning something new. I'm assuming I got full points by agreeing to go on an archaeological dig, so no need to stretch into my discomfort any more, right? No jumping out of airplanes or eating raw octopus. I wonder if Domitia ever ate raw octopus. Definitely a *no* on the airplanes.

So, what I read last night is blazing through my brain as I'm reading this book that Lena brought over about Domitia, former empress.

"It brings me so much joy that we are all here reading about ancient Rome," Lena offers a broad grin from where she's perched on the window seat. She pops the textbook—it looks like a textbook—

back open and gestures at the page. "And I found something. Listen.

"It was rumored that Domitian's older brother Titus and Domitia Longina—"

"Sorry, that was her name? Lawn-*gee*-na?" Lauren asks. She snorts and looks at me. "I was pronouncing it 'lawn-JYE-nuh' in my head."

I let out a hoot of laughter, which is met with confused stares from Lena and Alessia, who apparently don't know all the words in English yet. Especially the words for female anatomy. "Never mind." I flip "go on" hands at her.

"OK. So, they were supposedly carrying on an affair. However, historians are skeptical. And, also, Titus died in 81 AD. Domitian became emperor after that, and that's when he would have gained control of the grounds here. It wouldn't have been convenient for Domitia because they were living elsewhere."

"Good point," I say.

"The major support that something was going on was in 83 when she was exiled. But Domitian invited her back soon after, either because he loved her or because he needed to put to rest the new rumor that he was having an affair with his niece."

"Ew," Lauren says. "Lots of philandering goin' on back then."

"What do you expect?" I say. "The aristocracy was marrying for alliances."

"Right, but banging your niece?"

"Yes, I would have drawn the line before that."

"I'm curious who Domitia was with," Alessia says. "Was she in love? Was she happy with him? Domitian took her away from her first husband. Maybe it was him?"

"This is the important part," Lena speaks sternly, clearly excited to get to the point. "Domitia had a cottage where she and her handmaids would go to rest and take a break from palace life. It was overlooking the lake and was known as Palatium Syreni, the Mermaid's Palace."

I bolt upright in my chair. "Wait. Do you think the mosaic of the fish that the one team has been uncovering on the floor could actually be a mermaid?"

"Exactly what I was thinking," Lena says. She places the book on her lap, her eyes sparkling. "I think we are uncovering the Mermaid's Palace. What if this is where Domitia met her lover?"

———

Sabrina was in bed with a headache that afternoon, while my team was in the library, but another team volunteered to make dinner, pick up groceries, and whip up a feast of local dishes. Thank God for Sabrina, she made sure the team knew my dietary needs ... without making it a *thing*.

If I could be adopted by the Zangari family, I would be a happy, if not somewhat chubbier, woman. Broccoli and skate soup, spaghetti and clams, and salads. So good. I was a little distracted during the soup course because all I could think about was when I found out the Croc Hunter had died—he was impaled in the heart by a stingray, which is like a skate (but they don't have stingers), while filming a special in Australia—and thinking that swimming with stingrays is definitely out of my comfort zone and will remain there.

Then I realize that everyone is buzzing.

Lena hasn't stopped talking to Dr. Rossi, who joins us with the happy announcement that we will be able to continue digging tomorrow. Neither of them has touched their dinner, which I happen to be wolfing down while listening to their excited chatter.

After Lena reveals our afternoon discovery, Ella excitedly claims that she too wants to be an archeologist, and also a romance writer, because it's so exciting.

"Ah, but Ella, you are going to join us at Pelletteria Zangari soon," Gianmarco says. "Only a couple more years, *bella*."

I feel like the food has lost a bit of its flavor as I realize the odd spot that Ella seems perpetually caught in, but she changes the subject.

"Do you have any fun Christmas traditions? Anything you do with your family?"

"Not really ..." I begin.

"What about your friends? What did you do last Christmas?"

Thomas ...

"Well, the year before last Christmas, I had just started dating someone, and I did some of his family's traditions with them. We went to this part of Pittsburgh called "the Strip," which is just a bunch of local shops and restaurants all on one street. We had to get everything fresh on Christmas Eve day for the Feast of the Seven Fishes, so we started at the fish market at 6 a.m. His aunt brought everyone really strong bloody marys. After we got all the food, we stopped by a coffee place where the employees were all tatted up guys who look like they make craft beer. The coffee was good, but ..." I catch Lauren's eye, and the look on her face nearly breaks my heart. I cut the story short. "Anyway, we did the Seven Fishes dinner with his family that night. Some of his cousins make wine, so they brought that, and it was really nice."

Lauren is staring down at her spaghetti and clams like all the chocolate in the world melted and ran down the drain.

"That's nice," Ella says. "We do that too. I thought Americans just liked gingerbread house competitions and stringing up enough lights on the house to cause a fire."

That gets a laugh from the table, and Lauren even manages a weak smile. My phone buzzes, and I see texts from both Mom and Declan. I'm not doing that right now.

"I haven't done any of that, but Lauren and I do have an impressive herd of reindeer in our yard."

———

Back in our room after dinner, I look at my phone and frown. My mom, of course, sent like ten texts checking on me because I didn't respond to the first one. She knows that I'm busy here and have an unusual schedule, but she just wants to be sure I'm OK. Oh, and can I stop by that bakery in the

Strip that has those rolls she got that one time in the late 90s when she did Thanksgiving with her mom's side of the family and was asked to bring rolls. I was like five. Of course I don't remember them. Is the store even there?

And Declan is checking about something his boys want for Christmas. Video game money and something for soccer and new art pens for drawing comic books. Sorry, *graphic novels*. I don't recognize the names of any of the video games. Yeah. I'm that old.

I respond briefly to both of them and add to my dinner and gifting notes on my phone.

Lauren went straight in the bathroom after dinner, and I'm giving her a little time. I know I said something that struck a nerve just by the way she looked at me ... and I can guess what it was about. We both have a complicated past ...

I check my email, too, while I wait. There's an email from Logan, this time to my personal email because I promised I would stop checking my work mail.

Hey Kenzi,

I was looking at Castel Gandolfo, which I discovered is *not* Gandolf's Palace from

Lord of the Rings, and now I'm less excited to get a postcard from there.

Kidding!

Have you visited any historic sites there besides the dig? I read about Palazzo Pontificio and saw pictures of the interior. Just curious if you got to go anywhere. I'd love to hear about it.

Logan

I chuckle at the Gandolf joke. Gotta appreciate the humor. Of course, I haven't been anywhere but the dig, the villa, and the village. I wonder if that's disappointing. I am in another country. I'm expected to go see some stuff. Have big experiences. Feel the ground shake.

I respond anyway. Maybe the food is still interesting. Everyone loves food, right?

Hi Logan,

Haha, Gandolf! Incidentally, he's staying in the tower down the road while the castle is being renovated. Orc attack. It happens.

I haven't been able to see any sites. It rained all day a couple days ago, and the ground was too soggy to dig today, but I spent the time in the library researching with my team. It turns out that we are all interested in history, architecture, and good stories, so it's a pretty good combination.

Dinner last night was amazing. Broccoli and skate soup, spaghetti and clams, and salads. They are local dishes. I was wondering about the skates though. Do they taste the same as rays?

Keep holding down the fort!

Kenzi

I never know how to end an email to a colleague. A friend? Are we friends since we've been emailing? I ponder the strangeness of the situation because we didn't talk much before, but it seems like we must be friends if he keeps responding.

I hope he doesn't think I'm odd. I delete the bit about the rays.

"What are you overthinking?" Lauren interrupts my thoughts softly from the doorway to the bathroom.

"An email to Logan."

"I see." She crosses her arms and remains in the doorway. "Work email?"

"No. I am being good. He has my personal email."

"Oh, personal. That's a step in the right direction for a couple reasons." Lauren manages a smile.

"Are you doing OK? I didn't even think about what I was saying at dinner—"

"I'm good. Just needed to process ..." She takes a long deep breath and lets it out slowly.

I grimace. "I see. Sorry, again."

"You had no idea." She waves her fingers to shoo away the thought. "I'm certainly not mad. You didn't do it on purpose. You helped me through one of the toughest times of my life. I don't think you would try to hurt me."

I nod. Flashing back to that dinner with Thomas and his family. Back when things were perfect and new. And possible.

I didn't know what to say. "Usually, you're the rational one with all the answers. Should I suggest that we meditate? Do some deep breathing? Should we write about what's bothering us and then burn it?"

"Ha. Ha." Lauren sinks onto the bed and makes a sour face.

I join her. "His family was always so kind, welcoming, and supportive. The past year, I've felt like I lost half of my village. It's depressing. I have you, of course." I squeeze Lauren's hand. "And some other friends. Grandma Claudia, a couple cousins I'm closer with now ... It's just that I got used to the extra love I was getting. And there is this empty place that wasn't just filled with Thomas but also his parents and siblings and the rest of them. When you break up, you lose more than just the one person and the safety and security they bring. It's like half your world falls apart."

"I know what you mean." Lauren is tearing up as she speaks, so then I start tearing up. Crap. I don't want to cry about him. "But you have to ask yourself if it's true. Do you really think that you lost all of that and the space that is left is just dark and damp and sad? Or do you think it's more like when a family leaves a hotel room, and the staff goes in and cleans the room, and then another family comes in?"

"That's quite a perspective." I think about it for a moment. "I like that a lot."

"I believe Jennifer Halliday refers to that as 'reframing.'"

"Luckily, I'm an architect. I already know a lot about building a house."

Chapter 9

We had a pleasant day on the dig site. Nothing interesting to report from the trenches, ha! We got to chat a little bit, enjoy the fresh air and the intoxicating smell of the lemon trees. Overall, it was nice! After dinner, I decided to walk to town to at least explore the outside of Palazzo Pontificio and pick up some postcards at a local shop.

I wish Lauren had come with me, but Mr. Eyebrows asked her to join him for a coffee as we were heading out, so I told her to go and that I would be fine going by myself. I mean, I'm a grownup, so of course I'm fine. I can walk around in a strange country by myself and fake knowing how to speak their language without anyone being the wiser.

I don't see any postcards when I walk in, so I think I will just ask. And now I'm pretty sure I'm just going to say, "*Mi scusi*" and leave.

"*Necesito una postal?*" I feel my face turning red as I struggle to communicate with the cashier. Why did I think I could ask where the postcards are? I should have just wandered around lost till I found them. I can feel my eyes start to burn as the tears get ready to spring into action. Why is it bothering me this much?

The cashier is giving me a puzzled look.

I can do this. I mime the shape of a postcard and writing on it, putting on a stamp ... "Postcard?" The guy has no idea what I'm talking about. Maybe I should say it with an Italian accent?

"Ha bisogno di una cartolina." A woman's voice behind me made me jump. I turn to see that Ella is smiling sympathetically at me.

"Ah, *cartolina.*" The gentleman gestures toward the corner of the store. *"Dietro quegli scaffali."*

"Perfetto. Grazie." Ella takes my arm and guides me away.

"Grazie!" I call over my shoulder. "What did he say?"

"Behind the shelves," Ella pauses and smiles like there is a joke. "And you were asking him for postcards in Spanish."

My face goes red again, and my throat tightens. "I am so embarrassed."

"Don't be. It happens more than you would think."

I'm human, and I make mistakes. I catch myself thinking about a line from the superpowers book, and I'm kind of proud of myself. Being in a country where I don't speak the language is really far out of my comfort zone, and I'm bound to screw up a lot here.

A man is unloading sodas into the refrigerated case near the postcards, and he smiles at us. People are friendly and forgiving. I'm good. They aren't judging me ...

I look at the postcards as Ella checks out some of the nearby touristy knickknacks. "Want to bring a palm leave in amber home to a friend?" she jokingly picks up the trinket and makes an "oh wow" face at it. I laugh. It makes me feel a little better.

"Che bei vestiti! Vai in un posto speciale oggi?" The soda man, who is incredibly handsome, is talking to us, and I have no idea what he's saying.

"He said our dresses are beautiful and asked if we are going somewhere special today," Ella quickly fills me in.

"Grazie," I say. I glance down at the simple fuchsia cotton dress that I've paired with a denim jacket and then back at him. I'm lost on how else to respond, so I just smile. Ella answers him, and the two start talking, so I just return to the postcards. A picture of the city from a drone ... a picture of the lake from the beach ... a picture of the palace ...

Would that be good to send Logan? Or is it weird because I didn't go in the palace?

And why am I so concerned about what to send him? Just pick something.

I hear them laughing then, and it warms my heart. I'm happy to see Ella happy, since she's had so much trouble with her boyfriend.

"Cos'è questo?" An angry male voice booms nearby, and I turn to see Edoardo. Crap.

The soda guy looks surprised, and Ella looks annoyed. She throws her hands up angrily. *"Non posso fare conversazione?"*

I step closer to Ella to support her, still clueless about what Edoardo is saying, but I know that she shouldn't be left alone to deal with this, even though, it's really not my business.

Edoardo is saying something and gesturing at the soda guy who holds up innocent hands and backs away. He grabs his dolly and heads for the door. Smart man.

I put my hand on Ella's shoulder and gesture questioningly at Edoardo.

"Kenzi, Edo thinks I'm flirting," she fumes. "He doesn't think I can talk to anyone without being unfaithful, for the love of God."

"Stay out of this," Edo says with vitriol. I'm taken aback, but I won't leave.

"No, you stay out of this. I was helping Kenzi find a postcard, and the soda man complimented our dresses. Kenzi doesn't speak Italian, so I thanked him, and we talked for a minute. What is your problem?" Ella's face is red with anger.

"I got you a coffee, and this is how you act?" Edo says.

"Sarebbe meglio che se ne vada, signore." I hadn't noticed the cashier inching closer to us as Ella and Edo argued. He crosses his arms. I also hadn't noticed that he's built like a bouncer.

"Me ne andavo comunque," Edo says. He thrusts a coffee at Ella, takes a few steps, and looks back at her.

"We are staying here," I say firmly. I sound brave, but honestly, I'm ready to cry. This guy is awful. And it's even worse when I'm trying to follow what's going on by tone of voice and body language. Geez.

Edo throws up his free hand and storms from the shop. For a moment, Ella and I just look at each other. Then I realize I still have some postcards in my hand.

"I should go pay for these."

When we get to the counter, the cashier says something to Ella, and she nods. He makes a face like he feels sorry for her. Ella says something else. Then, she looks at the coffee she's still clutching. "I don't even want this." She drops it in the trash can as we leave the store.

Outside, the sun is ridiculously bright, contrasting what just happened. It's still sparkling on the lake at the bottom of the hill, and there isn't a cloud in the sky. A light breeze ruffles our dresses and the nearby oleander. I still feel shaken up, so I can only imagine how Ella feels. Though, if she's used to this ...

Ella seems to have turned from anger to frustration or disappointment. I can't tell which. She's staring into the distance, completely glazed over, shoulders slumped. Her eyes are red, and as she places her sunglasses on her nose, she discreetly wipes a tear away.

I put my hand on her shoulder for a moment. Finally, I say, "Is there a good place here for gelato?" No sense being shaken and not recovering with excellent ice cream.

Ella shakes her hair like she's trying to get a fly to stop buzzing near her ear. "Yes, yes, of course. Down the street here. That sounds good." She fishes her arm through the handles of her tan leather purse, wipes at her cheek, and forces a smile my way.

A potted palm on either side of the door greets us, and we enter a small, dark *gelateria* at the end of a long line. "The line is good. All the good places have a terrible wait. If you don't have to wait, just leave. The gelato is probably awful."

I nod in answer and gaze at the case ahead of us. There must be a hundred flavors. Thank God the menu board has them in Italian AND English. I start to feel more grounded knowing what's going on around me.

"You OK?" I ask.

"Oh, this is normal. Edo is always doing this. We fight, and then things are fine."

"Ella." I pause. It's totally not my business, but I'm a few years older. I've been in crap relationships, but this relationship is basically a circus sideshow. I need to say something. "I don't mean to butt in, but you know, this isn't actually normal." We step forward as the line moves a smidge.

She looks at me but doesn't say anything.

"Have you seen other couples fight like this?" Maybe my definition of "normal" is different from hers. I can have an open mind. I guess. At least about what her experience is.

She chews her lip for a moment. "No." The line shifts again.

I take a different tack. "What are your parents like when they aren't with the rest of us?"

A soft smile lights her face. "Mama and Papa are so in love. They have a beautiful relationship. No one could treat Mama better."

"Is your dad ever jealous?"

Laughing, she says, "Absolutely not. They trust each other so much. Papa has to be gone a lot for business, and that wouldn't work if they didn't both trust each other."

"What about your brothers and your sister? I think your sister got married last year, right? What about your brothers?"

"Orlando is married, and Rico has a girlfriend. They aren't jealous like Edo." She sets her jaw, and I'm not sure if she's getting upset with me or maybe with herself. I nod.

We're close to the case now, and the brightly colored gelato looks like a mecca to me. For someone with celiac's, half the world of desserts is cut out because there is definitely wheat in it: cheesecake and pie have crust, cake, of course, and brownies, cookies, etc. It's aggravating to go to a birthday party, and I definitely avoid pub crawls. I'll have to ask if the gelato is safe, but there is a decent chance that it is. Except the cookie dough one. Clearly.

Ella points at a sign on the case, obviously reading my mind. "Gluten-free flavors are marked with an asterisk." I'm thrilled! Especially when I see that most of the signs bear a little star.

"You're in luck," Ella says. *"Dui gelati, piccoli,"* she tells the cashier. *"Uno cioccolato al peperoncini, uno al pompelmo."*

I probably could have stumbled through that myself, but I'm glad she took care of it. I can certainly say "two small gelatos" and maybe "grapefruit," since it's written on the label, but the one I picked, "chocolate pepperoncini"? That's a mouthful.

We grab a small table outside because the weather is perfect, and I get a mouthful of the gelato. I am definitely asking the Zangaris to adopt me. I could happily live off of this stuff. My gelato has the smooth, rich flavor of chocolate—*good* chocolate—that everyone loves with a little kick. It doesn't burn, but the chili enhances the chocolate flavor and reminds me a bit of those cinnamon candies that no one likes because they set your mouth on fire. It's a delicate balance to have the flavor not torch your mouth and overwhelm the chocolate. How have I lived so long without this?

It's a good five minutes before either of us says a word again because I'm still scheming how I can get Ella's parents to take me in so I can just stay here. And losing myself in the gelato.

"It must be good," Ella finally says. "You look like nothing in the world matters but eating all the gelato." She cracks out a laugh.

I smile. "Do you remember Julie? She's a little older, graying hair, from England."

"Yes, she's amazing. I can't believe she's doing this and she's blind."

"Right, her. We were talking a few days ago, and she mentioned that she wants to fall in love with a place and feel the way the ground vibrates because of what's there and what's been there. What matters. She said it's different to travel now because she doesn't get to *see* the places, so she *feels* them. She was telling us about Stonehenge ... you know Stonehenge?"

"Yes, of course."

"Right. And she said that she could feel a hum there that told her the power and the importance of the history and what those stones stood for."

"Mmmm. I love that. What a remarkable woman. I never thought about how a place feels."

"I hadn't either. But I'm fairly certain that I can feel the ground humming right now because of the power and importance of this gelato." I'm half serious, and actually a little drunk because of how good this gelato is. Ella shakes her head and laughs.

"It's holy gelato. Blessed by the pope. And it makes the ground move." She keeps laughing, and I realize that she took the joke somewhere that I don't understand.

"The pope blesses the gelato?" Maybe he does. Sounds legit.

"I'm so sorry. He doesn't really." She points up at the sign above the shop, Papa's Gelato. "'Papa' means 'father,' but it also means 'pope.'"

Cori Wamsley

My jaw drops as I catch on. "Ha! That's pretty good!" My phone pings in my purse, and I pull it out to see if it's important. "It's my brother."

Declan sent a text about a mile long about Sarah, his wife, wanting to make a traditional Lebanese Christmas dish: kibbeh. And she wants to know if we can have turkey or chicken instead of ham. It just wouldn't be Christmas with a ham, according to Sarah. And honestly, they never do ham.

Declan: Why did you pick ham? Turkey or chicken will go better with the kibbeh anyway.

It's my freaking house! I'd love to do sushi!

Also, I wonder if I can get some blessed gelato for Christmas dinner …

"You look stressed. Is he OK?" Ella puts her hand on my arm.

"Yes, he's fine. It's just … Christmas."

She smiles. "Oh, families all over the world are fighting about that right now. What's going on?"

"The menu," I deadpan.

She laughs and makes a face. "This year, my sister is taking a stand. My parents always make

154

manicotti, but she wants spaghetti with clams. Personally, I would love lasagna."

"I wouldn't be picky about any of that." I laugh. I've been so happy to have good gluten-free pasta that I would eat my weight in lasagna or whatever is put in front of me. Maybe I should rethink moving here ...

"It's tough leaving room for dessert, but I always manage. Mama makes the best tiramisu."

"Ohhhhh, I would love that." Suddenly, I prickle. There was something about dessert that I had to remember. I needed to write something down. But what was it. I frown.

"So, what about that book I've seen you reading? What does it say about persistent relatives with their food requests?"

I shake myself out of the reverie. I'm not going to remember right now anyway. "Ms. Halliday says that we can do brave things every day. I imagine she means not blocking Declan's number." We both laugh at that. I toss my cup in the trash, and we head back toward the villa.

Ella is strangely quiet on the way back, and I imagine she's just enjoying the pristine evening till I catch her with one eyebrow wrinkled. She's clearly deep in thought. "You OK?"

"Thinking about brave new things ..."

When we get back to the house, I give Ella a quick hug. "Thanks for saving me back there! That was perfect timing." I smile warmly at her. If you're ever going to stumble through Spanish-Italian, it's best to have someone nearby to save your butt.

"Thanks for saving *me*," she says. She turns quickly away, but I see the tears in her eyes right before she rushes off to the kitchen.

———

Day 11 and 12 have been fairly quiet. Alessia found some pottery shards all in the same area, so they are likely from the same pot. Dr. Rossi asked an intern to start piecing it together, and I think that would be the worst job. I don't have the patience for that. I can do easy puzzles, but nothing like a Rubik's cube, and this totally sounds like that. *Does this work? Does this work? Does this work?* Holy moly, I'm glad I'm just a digger.

Our group has been quiet, which is nice. I try not to think about the impending doom that is Christmas dinner at my house, and instead just push down the feeling of dread, which I know isn't healthy, but that's all I have going for me right this second, and I'm good at pushing down feelings. So, I do it like a pro.

I haven't found anything in my little pile of dirt, so I spend a lot of time between tiny shovels full gazing at the progress of the mosaic on the floor. It looks more and more like a mermaid, but I'm not sure if that's just because we got all excited about this place being the Mermaid's Palace.

What are you hiding, little old house? Was an empress meeting her boyfriend here? How disappointing would it be if she was actually just coming here to hide because palace life was really annoying, and she was tired of feeling pressured? What if this is just her secret hiding spot where she sat around reading books and thinking about how a couple thousand years from then, people would be digging around trying to figure out what happened here?

What if she busted up the pottery and the necklace and whatever else before she died and laughed because she was sending us all on a wild goose chase? Here's some old beads and chunks of pottery to entertain the future people!

I wonder if they thought that civilization would still be here. I wonder if they ever thought about it at all. Or if they were just living and doing their best every day.

I wonder if they had to read scrolls or tablets about living their best life.

Probably not.

"What are you smiling about?" Lena says. She's holding a lump of dirt between her fingers. She examines it, squeezes, and then drops it. "Rock," she says when she sees that I'm watching.

"Just thinking about what they were thinking about during Domitia's time."

"Mmmmm." Lena brushes the dirt from her hands and shifts to stretch out her legs. "They were probably thinking that they needed more griffin skeletons."

"No, YOU are thinking they need more griffin skeletons." I laugh.

"Tell me about it. Almost two weeks, and nothing."

"Sometimes the treasures we seek aren't the treasures we need." Julie smiles, places a hand over her heart for a moment, and continues digging.

I hadn't realized how close Julie's group was to ours, but she definitely heard us.

"I needed that. Thanks Julie." Lena lies back so she can reach Julie and touches her arm in appreciation.

"There are other good things about the dig. We've made new friends." I catch Lauren slyly glance in the direction of the crew working on the floor. "Had a new experience."

"Yeah," Lena's voice drifts off as she gazes at the team under Dr. Rossi's direction in the discovery tent. "Definitely some good things."

———

After dinner, I decide to take some time to myself. I grab my postcards and the superpowers book and walk to the beach. I probably have an hour till sunset, but there's still enough light. So, I want to make the most of it. I see Lauren bundled in her favorite beige slouchy knit sweater and jeans, walking hand-in-hand with that guy with the eyebrows ... Ernesto? They are in the lemon grove, and she looks really happy. I wave when she spots me and hold up the book. She gives me a quick thumbs up before returning to her conversation.

I brought an afghan from the room, and when I arrive at the shore, I sit in one of the Adirondacks, nestling into the blanket's warmth.

I decide to dive into *Trusting Your Superpowers* first because I've had a lot of time to reflect on the previous chapters I read. I need some new material to obsess over and figure out why I can't feel like *the goddess I am*, as the author likes to say. I suppose a goddess would be more amped to design the headquarters for an international fashion brand instead of feeling vastly inadequate in the skills department to handle the job. Actually, a goddess would inspire someone to do it for her.

I *don't* have that in me.

Tonight's chapter has the inspiring title "Feel the Fear." Like I'm going to do something else with it. Smell the fear? Taste the fear? What does that taste like? Rotting meat?

Then I catch myself.

So, right now, what I'm doing is procrastinating or avoiding doing what I'm supposed to be doing because there is some sort of fear in reading about how to change my life because, ahem, change is bloody scary.

I know this now because ... I've been reading this book. And examining my "superpowers," which is making me question literally everything in my life.

How did I get here? Maybe I should actually read the "Feel the Fear" chapter. Ugh.

Let's see what she says.

I stared blankly at my husband. Fear welled up inside of me. My hands were sweating. My stomach churned.

So far it sounds like that one Eminem song.

He told me he was leaving. He had a girlfriend. He wasn't happy with me. With our life together. And that's when I knew that I was terrified. I wasn't happy either, but I was staying. Was it brave that he hooked up with someone else and then decided to leave? No. Not in the least. But I wasn't being brave either. Frankly, we were both feeling the fear, and it took a third party for us to move on without each other, into the unknown.

That's something big that many people experience. We feel the fear, and we run back to the safety of the known. Women and men, every single day, stay in unhappy marriages, shitty jobs, and towns that don't align with what they want because it's less scary to stay there. "The devil I know," right?

If we take just one small step, though, it's less scary.

He packed his bags. I packed mine. We sold the house. We moved on. That all didn't happen in one day. It took weeks. But in our minds, we see the beginning point and the end point, and we freeze. We think that because the distance between the two is great, that the path will be painful. Beautiful soul, it isn't. It doesn't have to be. You don't have to quit your job and create a Fortune 500 company in a day. You don't have to go from grieving widow to happily married again in a day. You don't have to move across the country and reinvent yourself in an instant.

Take your time. But take those steps.

What are you really afraid of?

I close the book. My mind swirling.

My immediate response to the question would normally be "spiders" because it's funny and true. But I know that this is an invitation. And that in itself is scary.

What am I *really* afraid of?

I close my eyes and just ask the question into the chasm of my mind.

"Breaking things" is the immediate response. Breaking things.

I'm not that clumsy. I wonder why ...

Maybe it's not just things literally breaking. Maybe it's ruining.

Oh, now I'm getting a whole cascade of things.

"Kenzi! Be more careful. I can't believe you broke my grandmother's vase. You're always dancing where you're not supposed to!" – Mom, when I was little

"Kenzi, you ruined everything. You just had to keep your mouth shut, and no one would have gotten in trouble." – A "friend" in middle school

"Kenzi, why did you complain about your grade? Now we all have to retake the test!" – A classmate in my sophomore social studies class

"Kenzi, why did you choose to stay local for college? We could have both gone to California and had an adventure." – My high school boyfriend

"Kenzi, you left the presents in the living room. You *knew* Jenna was stopping by to study. Now you blew the surprise party." – My college roommate

"Kenzi, you really should apply to some larger firms. Your career could really take off if you were downtown. I bet you'll like it." – My advisor

"We can't get pizza because of Kenzi." – One of the other interns at the architecture firm where I interned, downtown, a firm that I incidentally *didn't* like.

"Kenzi, you just didn't get me. This is really on you." – Thomas ...

Wow, I'm afraid of being a ruiner.

I'm afraid. And I have all this "evidence" that I ruin things. So, I'm just trying to hide from any new experiences.

And Miranda wants me to do a *big* new experience. OK, Jennifer Halliday, let's hear how we fix it.

This isn't something you can fix just by reading this book.

Well then why the heck did I read it?

It takes retraining our brains to get us used to sticking our toe in the water, wading in, and swimming, even if the water is a tad cold.

The truth is that we need to build our feel-the-fear-and-do-it-anyway muscle every day so we can stretch beyond our comfort zones and reach our full potential.

Swimming, stretching, got it. Triathlon time.

Start by not *second guessing yourself. Listen to the little nudges and start trusting them. You know what's best. You know what direction to head in.*

When you feel like you should do something, don't shush that voice.

Often, we are taught to do things that we don't like and push down the urge to stop. Like sitting in a lecture where we are bored. We need it for credit. No one likes that professor. It's only for a few months. This sort of training means that we are also less likely to take the leaps that we know deep down that we need to take.

Dump that guy. Apply for that job. Say hello to someone new. Ask a colleague for help.

Those urges are our gut, our intuition, God telling us to move our butts ... whatever you need to think of them as to take action.

So, what is my gut telling me? Right now, it's telling me to pause because, wow, that was a lot of information.

Plus, the sun is sinking lower in the sky. It will be hard to see soon. Maybe I should write a postcard.

I'll be brave and do Logan's first.

Hi Logan,

> I had the best gelato yesterday: chocolate pepperoncini. It's like chocolate with a kick. I could eat it every day! It was truly wonderful!

Then I pause. Am I gushing? Who says, "truly wonderful"? So, Ms. Halliday jumps into my head and gives me a little shake. Why am I second guessing myself? Clearly, that's what I wanted to say, and it's fine.

Why worry? He asked for a postcard, and he gets what he gets.

I'm not a ruiner.

> One of my dig partners is hoping we find a "griffin skeleton," which isn't really that but rather a collection of bones cobbled together to look like one because that's what they believed it was at the time. Pretty interesting, right?
>
> Kenzi

And that's good. Plus, the picture of Palazzo Pontificio on the front is gorgeous. That's the side people always pay attention to anyway.

I jot a couple notes on postcards for Mom and Stan, Grandma Claudia, Dad, and Declan's family. I don't need to second guess those, and I actually realize why. I know them. I know how they will react. I know that my nieces and nephews will love the picture of the lake and flowers and that Dad will appreciate my joke that I'm "Roman" all over the area. I guess I don't know Logan very well, so I am overthinking.

J. Hall in my head again.

That doesn't have the ring I had hoped it would.

Satisfied, head still swirling, I hop up and start back toward the villa ... because my gut told me that it was snack time.

Chapter 10

After almost two weeks of digging, the site looks vastly different from when we arrived. Much of the floor in the main part of the house has been uncovered. The mosaic that we initially thought was a fish was indeed a mermaid. The wall across the floor from where my group is digging appears to have an irregular window or chink of some sort. Maybe the wall crumbled there. The table with a few pottery shards and bones is now covered, and a second table added. A handful of thin, fragile coins with a man's face are piled together. There is a small gold container decorated with a leaf pattern that Dr. Rossi said probably held makeup like kohl for a woman's eyes. We wonder if it was Domitia's.

Also, some of the artifacts have been carbon dated, and they are definitely first century AD, so the time is right for Domitian's rule. The pair were definitely in charge at the time, so they could have been using the villa here. Which means that everything we are finding could have been theirs.

A small group of us is eating breakfast outside near the site. We pull folding chairs close together to talk and enjoy the beautiful morning. The sun has somehow managed to warm the air to 60, and the smell of lemons mixed with the nearby oleander is heavenly. *Also*, they had gluten-free *cornetti* this morning, so I'm pretty happy anyway. I'm having a hard-boiled egg and a fresh pear from the garden with it, along with a raspberry spread that Sabrina made. Amazing.

As I sip my coffee and listen to the group chatting, I still can't believe I'm here. Work is a million miles away, though the thought of work brings back that jittery feeling that I'll be starting the Divya Shanti project in less than a month. I'm actually wearing one of her "Favorite Vs" today, a white V-neck top with bold red and purple hibiscus all over with my purple lightweight jacket. "Love your life" is scribbled across the front of the shirt, which I typically find inspiring but am realizing more and more that it can feel weighty, demanding.

What do you know about my life, Divya? I guess I chose the shirt, though.

I'm interrupted by Dr. Rossi, who pulls up a chair beside Lena. "Did you see the coins group five found yesterday?" I want to hug him for speaking in English any time he's around a mixed group of diggers.

"Ciao, Tore, I did," Lena says. Apparently, she's calling Dr. Rossi by his nickname now. How cute! "The one with Minerva and the spear is particularly well preserved. I'm amazed. Barely any wear at all. I wonder if it was even used."

"You're right. It doesn't look like a circulated coin would. It's like a perfect imprint. Probably lost soon after minting."

I can't help but think about Domitia here with a handful of fresh coins. Her husband's face on all of them. Feeling the weight of him and his reign and the fact that she didn't desire the marriage to begin with. Did she ever fall in love with him?

Soon after, we part ways, but Lena and Tore linger to talk. Then we are digging again.

The hours go by with some chatter from the groups. I'm still enjoying the warmth of the day, and the breeze begins wafting a smell from the kitchen ... maybe ribs. That's what Alessia says. Cooked in a tomato sauce. Doesn't sound like what I'm used to, but it smells amazing.

Close to lunchtime, a clink comes from a nearby trowel. Lauren says "Oh!" and we all look to see what she's doing.

I don't see anything.

She is now taking turns with a small pick and a brush trying to free whatever she found. It doesn't look like much. In fact, I think it's a rock. But we all look on excitedly to find out if it's something more thrilling.

A gold rim emerges. Then a dirty stone. I think it's red, but it's mostly brown and foggy from filth. All four of us are reaching in with brushes to see what it is, when Lena grabs a pick and starts working on the end that isn't as exposed. She's rewarded when links of a gold chain emerge. Finally, something intact!

We work on it for well over an hour, with all four women in my group close together. I can hear them breathing and see excitement dancing in their eyes. This is what we came for! I mean, Lena came for griffin skeletons, but this is probably a close second for her.

Eventually, Lauren is able to lift the precious necklace from the ground. It is completely perfect, which is shocking. I'm in awe.

"It looks like jewelry from their time. This is definitely old," Lena says. "2,000 years ago ..."

"I can't believe we found this!" Lauren says.

I see her eyes well up with tears as she gazes at the necklace in her hands. I get it. This is huge! I keep getting these feelings that I can't even explain, like we're walking where important people of the past walked, and it gives me this little tingle in my stomach. It's like *we're* part of history. It's unreal to feel that. Like I could reach out and touch those people of the past. To think that I have something in common with them, to have walked the same paths as them ...

Then, she rubs a finger across the smooth surface of the stone, and a shadow crosses her face. Lauren suddenly looks like she's a million miles away, and I know ... I just know where her mind has gone.

I put my hand on her arm and smile, "I feel it too." We've talked about it before. The elation, the excitement, the sweetness of the original memory ... and then how it was all dashed to pieces like the busted-up pottery we keep dredging up.

She shakes her head and forces a smile. "I'll take this to Dr. Rossi. I'm still in disbelief!"

"This is so amazing!" Alessia says. "Not a crack in the stone, intact chain. I can't imagine how often this happens. It is probably worth a fortune."

She didn't seem to notice the moment that passed between Lauren and me.

As Lauren scampers off, I brush the corner of my eye with the back of my hand. "Do you think it's just glass? Or a real stone?"

"Because this was probably a royal villa, I'm guessing that it's a ruby or garnet," Lena says. "It was common for them to set both stones like that.

They believed that garnets could protect warriors from injury when they went to battle and could protect everyone from plagues. They thought rubies could heal anything to do with the heart."

"Like the actual heart or like a broken heart?" I ask. My mind drifts back to a ruby that is more familiar to me ...

"Both," Lena says. "So, it could be meaningful jewelry ... or it could just be another pretty thing. Not everything needs to mean something."

I glance at Lauren, who is excitedly talking to Dr. Rossi. His mood likely rubbed off on her. He looks overjoyed, and he's motioning for an assistant to come over. Dr. Rossi takes the necklace and starts talking to the assistant, who jots notes down. The tent is becoming an exciting place!

I may need to send out more postcards!

Cartolinas? That's not right ...

As I return to digging, my mind wanders brazenly into the past. I find myself reviewing that more familiar ruby, against my better judgment.

"Rubies are for true love, so I wanted to get you this."

In the memory, I smiled. My heart was pounding away furiously in my throat as I gazed into his eyes. I felt so safe, loved. This was what forever felt like. This was what happened when soulmates found each other. It was like two beating hearts became one.

I looked down at the box. It was small, square, but not the shape of a ring box. A little bigger. I tore the paper and found a black box inside with the name of the jewelry store, Madison's, in gold script at the bottom. When I opened it, I immediately loved what was inside. It was a silver chain with an infinity symbol. At the bottom right of the curve was a heart-shaped ruby.

It was sweet.

"Do you want to put it on?" He seemed as excited as I did. That little flutter in my stomach when I met his eyes again told me that this was so right.

I know, it's just jewelry, but I was blissful. We were in love. It felt perfect.

Till it wasn't.

I still remember what Lauren said when she saw it.

"I hope it doesn't turn out to be a piece of junk."

"What?" I return to reality and see that Lauren had returned to our group with a frown.

"Did he think it was?"

"Dr. Rossi didn't say," Lauren says. "But once we cleaned it up better, I saw that it wasn't faceted. That stone might just be glass."

"Rubies in the Roman Empire were not faceted," Lena says. "They would be rounded, smoothed for fitting into jewelry, so no worries. I think you found something rare and beautiful."

"I wonder if it was a gift for Domitia, like we read about," Lauren says.

"I wonder if it is supposed to be for true love," I say. I didn't need to say anything. I mean, I probably shouldn't have, especially in front of everyone. Lauren caught my eye and raised an eyebrow.

"Rubies always are, aren't they?" she says dryly.

The chill in the air after that comment makes everyone shiver, and we all return quietly to our trowels.

———

The following day after lunch, I decide to read a bit and check my emails before returning to the dig. The back deck of the villa is the perfect spot to relax and take care of a few things privately. There are chairs, but not a great view of the lake, since it's to the front, so diggers don't usually break back here. What it does have is warm sun, a light breeze, and lovely landscaping. The pines that Italy is famous for stretch their arms toward the sky off into the distance. Flowers dot the spaces between, along with long grasses. I can see other villas and smaller residences down the hill toward another town that appears too far away to walk. I feel like I'm gazing into a painting instead of looking at the world around me. It's surreal in every direction.

I smash the floral print pillow a bit for good lumbar support—which immediately makes me feel old because I thought about it that way—and sit down in one of the handmade wooden chairs. I probably have another 30 minutes of break, so I can definitely get in a chapter and a few emails.

I start with email. Nothing but sales notices from stores and one email from Logan. He's excited about a great gingerbread recipe he found. He said it tastes just like his grandmother's recipe, which somehow didn't get passed to his family before she passed. He's "really psyched" about finding this recipe, and he tried it out with his nieces and nephews, which I find adorable. Apparently, everyone was thrilled!

Before responding, I want to think about what to tell him about. This place has been pretty exciting lately! So, I set my phone down and pick up my book.

"Ready to own my superpowers," I mutter. Today's chapter is about "abundance mindset"— whatever that means.

As it turns out, it's pretty important. I read on to discover that I need to stop being afraid that there won't be enough of something—money, food, parking spots, whatever—and just "believe" that there is always enough of everything to go around. Which makes me nervous about running out of stuff. Did I need to worry about these things? I better start. Or stop. Ahhhh!

But I love the example she uses.

Women often say things like, "All the good ones are taken," when they are dating and seem to always end up with jerks. That kind of thinking is going to continually land you with jerks, which does NOT align with the goddess that you are. Goddesses, dear sister, don't date jerks. They date men who are just as empowered as they are, who are worthy of our love and trust. Jerks, not so much.

On the other hand, believing that there are plenty of good men in the world for all the women who are searching for them means that you won't 1) settle or 2) get frustrated and give up, buy 20 cats, and become a man-hater. Abundance mindset, dear sister, means that you get what you want, your friends get what they want, your neighbor gets what she wants, and even that girl at work who you don't really care for gets what she wants because we live in an abundant world where everything just works out for you.

In fact, say that with me, "Everything just works out for me." And you better believe it!

Oh, ho! That could really change some thinking if I wasn't already verging on this-is-a-load-of-bologna-because-I-already-swore-off-men. I didn't really, but still.

Of course, if Lauren says that this book is for real, maybe I could try. People also say, "There are a lot of fish in the sea," so maybe ...

"Arrrrgh!"

I jolt upright at the sound of serious frustration that has just broken through my ridiculous thoughts about this book. Ella has just burst onto the porch, and she looks pissed.

I bookmark my page and smile kindly at her. She slumps into the chair beside me, crosses her arms, and stares not only daggers but also cleavers, swords, and many, many other sharp, dangerous objects into the poor, innocent flowers and trees around us. Mental note: do not cross this woman.

"Ella, you OK?"

She snaps to face me, and pulls her braid over her shoulder, rubbing her hands down it like a worry stone. "It's Edo."

Of course. "Do you want to talk about it? What do you need right now?"

Ella sighs and looks deep into my eyes for a moment before answering. "I do want to talk. I'm so angry." She throws her hands in the air and then pulls her legs up into the chair, resting her chin on the knees of her wide-leg black chinos. "He said he doesn't like Nico working here because we're too friendly. I've known him a long time. But Edo says he doesn't like the way Nico looks at me with puppy eyes. He does NOT look at me with puppy eyes. We. are. friends." She groans again.

I shouldn't say anything. Or should I. Maybe it will help? Why don't I have a script?!

I give a stiff laugh. "He actually *does* look at you with puppy eyes, Ella," I say. Good grief, what am I thinking?

For a moment, Ella looks bewildered. She puts her hand to her chest. I'm struggling to read her emotions. Good? Bad? Is she going to stab me? That look!

"Oh," is all she says. Then she goes back to stroking her hair.

"It doesn't really matter if he does. Edo shouldn't go off on you for it. I don't understand why he doesn't trust you."

"Edo is just Edo. He's passionate about us." Now she's defending him.

Abundance mindset ... "What do you think would happen if you told Edo that he can leave? What if you just said, 'If you think you can't trust me, then we're done.'? I'm not saying you have to ..." Why the *hell* am *I* giving relationship advice?

Ella frowns. "I don't want him to leave me. I love him." Then she starts sobbing. Oh boy.

I drop my stuff and pull my chair in front of her. "Hey, I'm sorry. I don't want to upset you. I was just thinking that you don't seem very happy with him. You're usually mad at him. If he can't stop being so jealous, then it doesn't sound like a productive relationship. Do you actually want to marry him?"

"Yes."

"So, here's a weird question ... what are you afraid of? If Edo isn't your boyfriend, then what does life look like?"

She sniffs and looks at me seriously. "I suppose I would just be focusing on my studies."

"Would you be happy?"

"I love school. I love reading. I suppose I could be. But I want my soulmate."

"Are you rushing? Forcing?" I pause and almost laugh. "I sound like my friend Lauren right now, the one with the red hair."

"Yes, I know her. She's really clever. Those are good questions." Another sniff, and Ella wipes her eyes with her sleeve. "I think I'm excited for what's next. My soulmate and then getting married and then kids and then growing in our careers."

"But what if this bickering continues? Do you want that while you are living through all those things? What if you have kids and go to a school function and speak to the gym teacher and Edo gets upset that you're flirting?"

A look of fear crosses Ella's face, and she scrunches up her eyes in a look that is painful. That future doesn't look good. "I hadn't imagined that far ahead with his behavior."

I pat her arm. "I get it. Sometimes we get so caught up in what's going on right now that we turn it into a fairy tale without examining the truth."

"What if he's the one? What if we can make each other better?"

"Two people can't make each other better unless they are both willing to be their best selves. And no one will change unless they want to." That totally sounds like Lauren. She will be proud of me when I tell her about this.

Ella gives me a quick hug. "Thank you. I needed this." Then she pulls out her phone. "You might want to head back to the site. It's almost time to start again."

"Thanks, I'll do that. Are you going to give this some more thought?"

She takes a deep breath. "I will. But I do love him."

"You don't have to figure it all out today," I say. "But I think it would bear some thinking." This isn't Ancient Rome. You don't have to stay in a bad relationship. The rules are different. In my head, the lines started to blur between Ella and Domitia, and I wondered if there was a way for Ella to just leave and be happy. We know the empress couldn't.

As I walk back to the dig site, I remember that I was going to respond to Logan, so I pull out my phone.

Hi Logan,

We found something amazing yesterday, so I wanted to share! It's either a ruby or a garnet in a gold setting on a chain. The whole thing was perfectly intact. It's like we just picked it up off someone's dresser. Lena said it's from the time of Domitian, so it likely belonged to his wife or someone else in the court.

We hope that Dr. Rossi will get us some information about it soon!

Gotta go dig!

Kenzi

I hit send, and a shiver tickles down my spine. I just dredged up a weird memory.

"Kenzi, we need to make four dozen cupcakes tonight for the bake sale."

"Mom, I have a lot of homework. I won't have time. And we did that for the last bake sale. It's someone else's turn."

"They are depending on us. I volunteered because no one else makes good cupcakes. You know that. Declan, I'll need your help too!"

"Track practice tonight, remember?"

"Oh shoot. I need to drop you off, don't I? Why don't they have a bus to take you to the high school?"

"Mom, you should complain about that. All my friends said their parents are annoyed too. It's an extra trip, and they have a lot going on too."

"I'm not going to stir the pot."

Why in the world did I just remember that? I'm almost back to my spot, trying to send an email as I'm walking so I can get there on time ... but what happens if I just take a minute to do what I need to do? Is that why I thought about that time in elementary school when we made cupcakes while I diagrammed sentences? What a horrific use of time, by the way. I've never needed that skill!

But we had to, right? Because my mom knew that no one else could. Or would. Maybe they all did a crappy job so Mom would do it. There's a lot to unpack with this one.

What did she get out of making the cupcakes every time? Feeling needed? Feeling important?

What would have happened if, just once, she let it go? It wasn't on her to make everyone happy or raise all the money herself or take care of it.

It was everyone's responsibility.

Oh shit.

So, it's not on me to find something in every dig of the dirt.

It's not on me to make sure the entirety of Divya Shanti's headquarters is built without a hitch.

And maybe it's not on me to completely control Christmas dinner because it's at my house.

Oh shit.

That's actually freeing. Maybe I can delegate and share responsibility.

What am I afraid of? I'm afraid that I have to take all the responsibility for everything and then feel like a failure if it's not perfect instead of thinking that everyone shared in the blame or success.

Thanks Mom.

I'm not responsible for everything. I feel like I should take a deep breath now and "exhale all the junk," as Lauren likes to say.

"Lauren, I had a major revelation." I flop down beside her in the dirt and fill her in on the lunch break happenings.

"That's pretty crazy about Ella," she says. "I wish we could just tell her to dump the guy, but she has to come to that conclusion herself. You did the right thing by asking her questions and letting her think. I'm proud of you."

"Thanks!"

"As for you ... you think all that people-pleasing is because you don't feel like you can rely on others to pull their weight because that's what you were taught? Or is there more?"

"Oh, there's probably more." I pull my legs up and wrap my arms around my calves. The sun flickers through a cloud and dances across the site. The floor team, a group of four men including the eyebrow guy, is laughing hard, slapping one of the guys on the back. Alessia and Lena are by the table with the artifacts, Lena chattering excitedly with Dr. Rossi again, as Alessia hangs back. Nearby, Julie is twisting her hair back and clipping it with a claw while she tells a story to the others in her group. They stare at her raptly.

The connections that we had woven over the past two weeks were strong, even if I had some apprehension before we left Pittsburgh. Already, everything has changed. Could more things change? Would I be able to let go of control? Would I be able to stop fearing control?

———

The next evening, most of the diggers returned to Giorgio's Beach for a bonfire. Ella brought some of her brother Rico's homemade limoncello—clear liquor with lemon zest soaked in it—and we all partook.

"This stuff is really strong!" I am overwhelmed by the force of the flavor, as well as the alcohol content. I make a funny bitter face, but it's not that bitter. It's just ... a lot.

"Tore, your students would laugh at you!" Lena doubles over cackling, and I look in her direction. Dr. Rossi tags along with us, hoping to share news of the carbon dating and some research one of his grad assistants is doing on campus as soon as it rolls in. At least that's what he says. Secretly, Lauren and I are certain that he wants to spend time with Lena, who he is sitting beside, and who hands him a shot of said limoncello as soon as he sits down.

Yes, I'm holding all my "carbon dating" jokes—two diamonds walk into a bar—inside because no one but me ever thinks they are funny. Especially people who actually need carbon dating in their jobs.

Poor *Tore* shudders with the strength of the liquor. Yep, his students would definitely laugh at him.

"How does anyone drink this stuff? It tastes like cleaner." He squeezes his eyes shut and looks like he is trying to exorcise a demon from his mouth without parting his lips.

Ella, about to do a second shot, chuckles. "Excellent! I'll tell Rico that he finally perfected the recipe!"

"We're guinea pigs?!" Lauren exclaims.

"Sorry, I don't understand." Ella shoots the drink and exhales a long, slow breath. She looks like she feels powerful after the second shot. No faces. No shuddering. Just letting it slip down her throat. Geez.

Lauren laughs. "I mean you were experimenting on us."

"Ah. No. Rico knows what he's doing. He tweaked the amount of lemon for this batch. It's so good." She makes the chef's kiss sign and giggles.

"I'm glad we got to try it and approve," Alessia says.

Lauren nudges me. "You can add this to the list of new things you tried this month. It's getting pretty long."

"You're right." Oddly, I hadn't thought much about it lately, but she is correct. "I don't think I've tried anything new in a decade."

"Oh my goodness, that's crazy!" Ella draws out the "a" in "crazy," so I assume she is feeling toasty from the limoncello. "What do you normally do? Just draw houses and sleep?"

A little part of me is indignant, but she's right. At least, I've done the best I can for the past year to draw houses and sleep, so I don't have to try new things. So I don't have to fail. Or break stuff. Uggggggh ... "Pretty much," I finally answer. I'm worry that I took a little too long to respond so they are going to ask me weird questions.

"Well, we are certainly glad you chose to join us for this wild adventure, aren't we?" Julie raises her shot glass of limoncello as a toast, and I realize that she's been sipping it slowly this whole time. Sipping it. Like she loves the bitter flavor and the way her throat burns as it goes down.

"Thank you, Julie!" I say. "It's been wonderful being here with you guys. I may need to make adventure more of a habit."

"That's what my Uncle Humph used to say, 'Make adventure a habit.'" Julie took another sip of the Lysol on steroids. "He would come in the house all tanned or carrying a big bag we had never seen, and we would ask, 'Where've you been, Uncle Humph?' and he would always tell us that he was on an adventure. That man did the most extraordinary things. Never had a normal job. Just set out on adventure after adventure. Worked on a cruise ship for a bit in the '80s. Flight attendant, farmhand, golf caddy, beekeeper, drove a car from the dealership in Germany to some Austrian nobleman's house, captured snakes in Africa for the zoo ..." Julie ticked off the odd jobs on her fingers.

"That's a lot of jobs!" Lena says.

"He was multi-passionate. But that's what he said kept his life from getting too boring and predictable. He made adventure a habit. He was gone a lot, but when he came to visit, he had the best stories. That's how I want to be. Not a lot of possessions, but damn, will I leave this life with a lot of stories."

"That's what I was thinking about when I decided I wanted to come here," Lauren says. "I wanted to have a good story. I wanted to have an adventure."

"You should," Alberto says. Maybe that's his name. Eyebrow guy. I should really ask Lauren again, but she's told me like three times. He pats Lauren on the arm, and I see his almond-colored eyes twinkle. He's with a group of men from the dig seated close to Lauren. Actually, I can't remember any of their names, but I know they said they are all from Italy. And most of them speak English.

Lauren smiles coyly at him, nodding. "I don't have any real reasons to stay put right now, aside from loving where I live. Why not take off and make memories?"

"Exactly," Julie says.

When did I stop being brave? I swear I used to be the first one in line for the diving board. The one to touch the frog in the garden while all the other kids screamed "Ew!" and "Warts!" OK, the warts thing made me squeamish, but it was less that the frog could actually give me warts because, come on, everyone knows that isn't true, and more that I didn't want anyone to think I *had* warts. I wanted them to think I was brave for touching the frog.

I play with my hair and wrap it around my hand, letting the strands slip through my fingers. I repeat the action over and over. "I wanted to come here because I've never been to Italy, Lauren was coming so it didn't seem so unreachable, and I needed something to get me back on track. I've been scared of new things lately. Something happened a few months ago that shook me, not in a good way, and I needed a good kick start."

"I am always available for a kick start," Lauren says. She leans over on the bench and wraps me in a huge hug.

But it was more than just the breakup with Thomas, and I realize that as we are hugging. It started a long time ago. Somewhere between the brave frog-touching little girl and the broken-hearted woman before last Christmas.

And then I remember. Declan and I were out riding our bikes. We weren't supposed to go off the trail, but we did it a lot. He was always pushing himself to do jumps. Nothing too crazy. And he knew how to fall. He always rolled, so the impact wasn't as bad. But that was the funny thing about Declan. He always *knew* he was going to fall before it happened. I wasn't that lucky.

Declan is three years older than me, which isn't big right now, but when you're little, it's huge. He was ten when I was seven. He was 15 when I was 12.

That's a big jump in maturity. In knowing the world.

And I was always trying to out-do him, for the love of pizza.

We were jumping our bikes in the park, off the trail, of course (don't tell Mom) when Declan slid to a stop. "Kenzi, stop. That's not safe." It was still weird hearing his big boy voice. It sounded more authoritative than just a year before.

"You did it."

"But I'm a lot bigger."

"Just because you're a boy, you think you can do everything, and I can't."

"You're little."

I stuck out my tongue and put my foot on the pedal, determined.

"Let's see if Mom will let us have ice cream after dinner."

"After I kick your butt!" I was nine. Today, I would definitely say "ass."

I pushed off the ground and found the other pedal, shoving it down hard as I sped toward the jump.

It wasn't all that high, maybe a couple feet, but I wasn't prepared at all for the landing. I panicked. And I tried to stop my bike too fast after I hit the ground. Because there was a pile of rocks too close, and I was skidding toward them. Then I was *in* them.

I felt a lot of things that I never thought about before. The burn of seriously skinned knees and elbows. The trickle of blood running down my arms and legs from all the cuts and scrapes. The throbbing on the left side of my head where I smacked off of a rock. This was before parents were adamant about wearing helmets, so yeah ...

What's bizarre was that I knew in my heart that I could do the jump, but I never thought about the landing, and after that, I stopped listening to myself when I thought something would be OK. I didn't know when to say, *yes, I know,* and *I can do this.* I was always squeamish, just like the other kids with frogs. But they eventually grew out of it, and I never did.

"I'm glad you wanted to come, Aunt Julie," Hugo says. "It gave me a chance to see new places too."

New places ... it doesn't have to be across the universe. Sometimes it's right in your backyard. New experiences happen all the time. Everywhere. And you have to take brave steps forward to achieve them. Always. No matter what. It's scary, but it has to happen, or you just sit there wondering what it's all like and being too afraid to move.

"And I'm glad I have you to adventure with." She pats her nephew on the knee and grins. "I'm teaching a new generation the joy of new experiences, of stretching your limits beyond what was possible yesterday."

But when you don't believe that new things are possible, you stay put. You build walls. You don't go forth and explore or conquer or anything. You just ... stop. And it hurts, but it's also safe. You stay curled up in a ball so long that you ache for more.

This is the more.

This is the now. This is where I know I need to be so I can finally take a deep breath and soar.

This is how I learn to trust my gut again.

"If I didn't know in my heart that doing something new was still possible, I wouldn't have been able to *feel* Rome and Castel Gandolfo. I wouldn't have been able to *hear* the birds and touch the soil and all the artifacts here. I wouldn't have been able to *taste* the lemons in the air and smell the leather and the tobacco and the unique scent of Lago Albano. I bet you didn't know there is a tobacco farm to the west. I do." Julie taps her nose and laughs. She sips the limoncello and breathes out the contented sigh of a woman who is in control of her life and is involved in every tiny experience of it.

"Sure, sometimes I fall, but it's OK to fall," Julie says. "I've fallen a million times."

"I'll never tell," Hugo laughs. Julie wraps an arm around him and rubs the top of his head, affectionately messing up his hair, which has the rest of the group cackling.

I notice Ella then. Her huge brown eyes flickering from the bonfire. And she looks like she is rapt with attention. She needs to hear this. Whatever it means to her, Julie is clearly speaking a deep and powerful truth. Ella's lips part, and then she mouths, "Oh," and I know she's taken something to heart. Still absorbed by the spell that Julie is weaving, she places her hands on her lap and leans forward.

"I know that people pity me because I've lost my eyesight, but I haven't lost the world. And many people have. Living is about savoring every moment. About seeking joy on your terms. About following your rules and being ruled only by your heart. It's not about compromising yourself because someone else tells you that's the way it has to be."

Tears in her eyes, Ella leaps to her feet and abruptly walks off toward the lake. She slips off her shoes and wades in the water, letting it lap at her ankles, and suddenly, that seems like the most natural thing in the world to be doing right now.

I need to connect with the water, to feel a part of this part of the world.

I glance around for Lauren and see that she's already peeled off her shoes and is walking through the water a good distance from our campsite, an arm around ... Antonio? He says something and stops, wraps his arms around her. Then their lips are locked, and his hands are tracing her back. Hmmm. I'm happy for her.

I slip off my shoes and jog to join Ella at the lake. The manmade beach is soft, and the sand sinks between my toes. I feel tiny pebbles and sticks buried in the sand as I pad to the shore. There, I'm suddenly drenching my feet in chilly water that feels like it could cleanse away any of my worries. I glance at Lauren and her guy and chuckle to myself. She probably needed that.

Between the power of Julie's words, the limoncello, and the beautiful camaraderie, I feel every single thing around me: the wind, the joy, the peace. I smell the lake, for real, for the first time since I arrived ... along with the lemon, but probably not the tobacco. I do notice the earthy smell wafting from the dig site. Our dig site. And I feel so at home that it hurts.

Chapter 11

It's day 16, and most of the group is dragging. Even if many of us didn't have too much limoncello last night, we did stay out at the lake pretty late. The crowd at breakfast is fairly quiet.

"I thought I would have some news from the carbon dating of the ruby necklace, but it's not in yet." Dr. Rossi didn't seem too affected by our late night, but he's also living on the adrenaline of a treasure hunt. I brush away the silly thought in my head of two chunks of coal awkwardly meeting at a restaurant for the first time. Carbon dating ... "However, it appears to also be from the same period as the other artifacts we've found, based on the design of the setting and the type of chain."

Lena turns to our group—seated together munching on fruit, hard-boiled eggs, and various *pane*—and applauds quietly. The bunch of us smiles. Tired, but happy, we know that this is a major find, and honestly, even though archaeology wasn't really my jam till I came on this trip, I was pretty excited about the discovery and what Dr. Rossi's team would say once they had their test results.

"Also, today, you may notice a helicopter circling the site," Dr. Rossi continues. "Don't be concerned. They are doing Lidar testing of the area. Lidar uses a remote pulsed laser to generate 3D information about the characteristics and shape of the earth's surface. It's usually used to detect old oil and gas wells so they can be sealed off to prevent carbon dioxide seepage, but in our case, they are looking for adjacent structures that could inhibit the Zangaris' construction project further or pose a danger to anyone in the area because they are unstable, though instability is unlikely."

"Basically," Lena jumps in, "Lidar can tell us if there are any other ruins in the area so we know if we can stop exploring beyond the walls of the small house we have been digging in. If there is nothing else, the Zangaris can finally build their event center."

The look between Dr. Rossi and Lena was unmistakable and adorable. Clearly, they *dig* each other. Ha! "You're correct, Lena."

After breakfast, we wander to the dig site and get to work. Dr. Rossi wasn't kidding about the helicopter. It circles all morning and is pretty loud. Lauren and I entertain ourselves a couple times by mouthing "What?" and "I can't hear you" while laughing, but we eventually just give up.

I didn't mention anything to Lauren about the guy she was kissing last night. She came back to the villa with us, hand-in-hand with him. And they parted ways for the night. Obviously, we all have roommates, so it's unlikely anything was going to happen that wasn't totally awkward. She looked a little distracted when we were brushing our teeth, but also, we were both drunk, so maybe it was the limoncello. Or our exhaustion.

Still, I worry about her. She's been out on a few dates this year, but nothing has really stuck. And she's always so upbeat. I guess after the incident, she's recovered well. OK, better than me. For a long time, it turned my stomach to think about men. As my phone vibrates, I'm suddenly reminded of a certain man I've been emailing with throughout this trip, though, and maybe, just maybe, my aversion is disappearing.

Still, though.

I'm pretty lucky to have Lauren to hang out with. After we first started hanging out, getting each other through that majorly rough patch, we were cemented as besties. I knew she was "the one" as far as a BFF goes. Totally gets my humor. Is cool with my introversion. Is continuously nagging me to better myself—all in fun of course—and sometimes I do. Which is one of the reasons I trusted her enough for me to come on this trip. It's been pretty amazing. Though my eardrums aren't thanking her right now.

As the helicopter loops away toward the lake, I think of something.

"Hey Lena, do you think the helicopter radar thing can pick up on anything large that may be buried. Like a large collection of bones. Or maybe a car."

"A buried car?" Lauren says.

"I was thinking of things from other times. It might be useful to find a car that's been buried."

"I'm not sure that it would pick up on anything like that," Lena begins. "It may sense the empty space inside the car if it's a big enough 'gap' in the area underground, sort of like a cave would be. Bones though, probably not."

"Ah. I was hoping it might find your griffin bones," I say.

Lena sighs. "I wish." Her Apple watch buzzes, and she glances down. Then a look of delight spreads across her face. "I have a book in on inter-library loan. There are only a few copies left of *Masters of their Fates: Roman Empresses and their Love Affairs*. Universitá di Studi Storici tracked one down for me and ordered it. It took a couple weeks, but it's finally here."

Alessia laughs. "So you ordered it as soon as we got here?"

"I did. And I'm very excited to get it," Lena says.

"Will *Tore* be picking it up for you?" I ask with a sly smile, emphasis on Dr. Rossi's nickname.

"I see what you're doing. He's a friend." But the way Lena's beautiful olive skin takes on a red tint tells me that she wishes he wasn't.

"That book has an interesting title," I decide to change the subject. "Is it a line from *Julius Caesar*? 'Men at some time are masters of their fates. The fault, dear Brutus, is not in our stars, but in ourselves, that we are underlings.' I think that's right. We had to perform that scene for one of my English classes in college, and I will *never* forget it."

"Clever." Lauren shakes her head and smiles.

"I know, right?" Lena says. "Masters of their fates ... I guess the empresses did what they could." She pokes at her watch and then returns to digging.

———

After lunch, I step outside to return with the group to our dig site, but Gianmarco stops me. "If you have a moment, I would like to talk."

My mind flashes back through everything from the past two weeks. Is he just now hearing about the broken pottery? Did he find out that Lauren and I wandered from the tour of the leather factory? Did I do something else?

Why does my brain immediately go to worst case scenarios? Deep breaths, Kenzi!

I smile. "Sure, now is good. What's up?"

He motions for me to follow him to the veranda at the back of the house where Ottavia is waiting with mugs of hot tea. There is a tray with sugar cubes, lemon, honey, and small cookies. "They are gluten-free, Kenzi." Ottavia smiles as she gestures to the tray.

"Thanks!" I clearly didn't do anything bad or they wouldn't be giving me cookies, right? Or maybe they would give me *regular* cookies and watch me squirm. I guess it's not about the pottery … I sit down with a mug and add lemon and sugar. I *had* to add lemon. I mean, there are lemon trees *right there*, so I know it's fresh.

"We want to talk to you about your ideas for the new event center." Gianmarco didn't look like he was joking. Instead, he is sitting forward in his seat, hands clasped around the mug, looking intently at me.

My throat immediately closes up. What? I'm just here digging ... I mean, I'm an architect, but ... me? "I would love to talk about it. I thought you already had a plan though." Somehow, my response sounds way cooler than I feel.

"We do ... but I like what you had to say before about adding the large windows to allow light throughout the center. We thought you may have more suggestions."

"Also," Ottavia begins, "we Googled you and your company. It looks like you're well-versed in green design. We want that so much for our building. But not only that, we want to work with the ruins, making them part of the beauty of the building. There has to be a way to carry over some of the design from the house and make it look like the event center belongs here. Like we intended to bring the past and present together. We want something unique and beautiful that blends both."

I slip my hand over my heart and lean back in the chair. This is seriously a dream project. There are so many things I can do with the mosaics, the mermaid especially, and the tilework. "Where will you be shifting the site to? Do you know when the results from the helicopter ... testing ... thing will be in?"

"We should have them tomorrow." Gianmarco looks pleased. I haven't committed, but my body language is pretty obvious. "So that's a yes, right?"

Do I want this? Yes. Can I handle this? Yikes! I don't know. I mean, probably. Yes. If I can have a team, I can do anything. To delegate ... not to check me.

"Yes. I would love to see the previous design and get the results from the testing once you have them."

Gianmarco half stands to reach me so he can shake my hand. He lets out a joyful laugh. "Ha! I'm overwhelmed with excitement right now. This will be so completely different from anything that is out there now. I can't wait to get started."

I sincerely can't either. I can picture the recycled glass used as mosaics on the front of the building. Echoes of the broken tile from the floor of the house that I work up the walkway from the parking lot and into the flooring of the stoop. The stucco style, a soft bone white to coordinate with the villa and the subtle neutral tones from the dig site. It's going to be beautiful.

———

That evening, Tore is kind enough to bring *Masters of their Fates* with him to the dig site. He had been at the university all day and was only joining the group after dinner.

After our delicious feast of lasagna and huge salads with fresh basil, Lena couldn't have been more excited to see him, but the book was of slightly higher importance. With a quick "thank you," she grabs it and starts thumbing through to the section she is looking for.

"Dr. Rossi, thank you so much for bringing this book!" Lauren says. "Did you want to look at it with us?"

Lena looks up immediately and reddens again. "I'm so sorry. Yes, thank you! I'm overly excited to read about Domitia. The table of contents is online with the listing, and there is a chapter about her. Would you join us? We were going to the beach to talk and read."

"Is there limoncello?" Dr. Rossi laughs.

"Not tonight." Lena gives him a twisted smile and a wink. "I know we were all too much for you already. Only wine tonight."

Our group of five sets off for the beach, carrying blankets for around the fire, since there is a chill in the air. And some wine and plastic cups.

Dr. Rossi sits beside Lena on one of the benches, and the other three of us crowd onto the adjacent bench and wrap a blanket around us. It's cozy. And it's comfortable in a homey kind of way. I never thought I'd come halfway around the world and make friendships that feel this close, but here we are. Oh, and the wine. We pour cups for each of us and pass them out as Lena cracks open *Masters of their Fates* to what I assume is the chapter on Domitia. It looks like she's going to read for a bit and then share what she finds, so the rest of us chat.

"What made you want to go into archaeology?" Lauren asks Dr. Rossi.

"It's hard not to be interested in archaeology because of where we live." He shrugs.

"I imagine. I would find it hard not to traipse off to museums every weekend if I lived here."

"Plus, all the cities surrounding the museums. Rome has been around since 753 BC, Napoli since around 600 BC, Florence since 59 BC. You can just wander around and see the history. It was pretty amazing as a child growing up here."

"We don't have anything that old in the US," I say. "It's so different over here. I can't imagine how I would be if I had grown up here instead. I'm sure I would have loved architecture still, but it would be … different."

"Oh certainly. We are all a product of our surroundings, whether we want to be or not. Every experience, every place, shapes us."

"Here it is!" Lena says. She had been leaning back, wrapped in a blanket with the book close to her chest. The blanket droops now, and she's on the edge of the bench. Dr. Rossi reaches over to pull the blanket back on her shoulders. "I'll just read it to you.

"Domitia was known to have a lover named Marius Tatius. He was governor of Latium et Campania at the time of Domitian's rule and also acted as a trusted advisor to the emperor when he was staying at the palace at Castel Gandolfo.

Domitia's maids often accompanied her to the far eastern end of the estate grounds where a private residence had been built just for Domitia to relax but still be close enough to the palace to have the full guard there quickly if needed.

According to lore of the time, Marius Tatius would visit the palace and then claim that he needed to walk the gardens to clear his head. That is when he would slip away to the private residence, known as Palatium Syreni, to consort with Domitia.

Often, after visits from Marius Tatius, Domitia would be seen wearing jewelry that she previously hadn't worn, which she claimed were family heirlooms. The Carbunculus Macedonicus was a favorite of hers, though it has been lost to time. This particular necklace had a striking red stone set in gold."

"Hang on." I'm thinking. What if I'm right? "Isn't a 'ruby' also called a 'carbuncle'?"

"I think it's just any red stone," Lauren says. "Rubies, garnets, maybe others. So you think we might have found the ... Carbunculus Madunculus?"

Lena laughs. "The Carbunculus Macedonicus. We might have!

"Emperor Domitian was particularly fond of his griffin skeletons. Because griffins were known to be protectors of gold and other treasures, the emperor was superstitious about their presence and insisted on several at the site of the Palatium Syreni. He believed that they would protect his empress from attack. Early in his reign, a group of Dacian warriors had crept into Rome and assassinated a senator before being captured. After this, Domitian became more superstitious and often required the empress to remain in the palace, even with her guards. The Palatium Syreni was her only escape for much of the rest of his reign.

"No griffin skeletons have been found in the vicinity of the Albanum Domitiani, however." Lena adds, "That's Domitian's Villa."

"So where are they then?" Alessia says.

"I'm disappointed," Lena says. "I know he had them in Rome, and I hoped they would be here too. Now where did they go?"

"Often, sites are looted, Lena," Dr. Rossi says. "We don't know what happened after Domitian's murder. His people might have taken the skeletons with them. Or sold them. Or Emperor Nerva took them."

"Who murdered Domitian?" I ask.

"Two praetorian prefects, some palace officials, and ... his wife were all in on it." Dr. Rossi opens his hands in a "ta-da" motion. His smile is grim. "He had it coming, apparently. He was in debt and started confiscating land and possessions from various people to cover the costs of his building projects and his army. When he executed his cousin, everyone realized that no one was safe."

"Not even the griffin bones could protect them," Lauren says.

"So, we managed to link the necklace with the lovers and the house where we are digging ..." Lena looks pensive. "I just wish we could find those griffin bones."

"Why are you so fascinated by them?" Dr. Rossi asks.

"What is there not to like?" Lena says. "Griffins were believed to mate for life, which is horribly romantic." Even in the firelight, I can see her color rising as she clears her throat and continues. "Ancient people claimed ostrich eggs were griffin eggs and Alpine ibex horns were griffin claws. They wanted a part of the magic so badly that they would believe anything. And emperors owned griffin skeletons. Sure, they were assembled from the strange fossils of dinosaurs and other creatures that were found in the dessert, but still ... there is just something about griffins that has made people for thousands of years pause and take notice. They try to be a part of the myth. They want to own it. It's a creature that they believed protected treasures. Really believed that. So many of the mythical creatures they recognized as something that was long gone, but the people of ancient Greece and Rome really thought they were living in the time of the griffin. I find that so fascinating that I want to see it. I want to not only walk in their footsteps and breathe the air they breathed; I want to see what they saw and believed."

What Lena said was so beautiful. It's one of the "feel the ground vibrate" sort of things. Truly feeling like you're part of this world. Which is something that I've felt less of over the years till ... this place. My eyes are open to the amazing things around me for the first time in so long. Before this trip, I was trying to push things away, to stay small. And now, I feel the smallness of myself in this big world and on this long timeline and don't feel so insignificant. I feel like I'm marking my place and taking up space, and I'm OK with that.

Really. I'm OK.

———

"Friendships blossom in the funniest places, don't you think?" Ella joins us at the dig on day 17 and is sitting with my group, scraping away at a potential relic. We tell her about Lena's inter-library loan that had us all excited last night, which I realize sounds ridiculous to people who don't get excited about history and romance and that sort of thing, but Ella totally gets it. In fact, she loves that we were all excited about it.

"It's interesting to me that people from all over the world can come together for a common cause and enjoy building friendships from that," Lauren says in reply. "I seriously want to come back to Italy again and hang out with all of you. This has been a wonderful experience, one that I'll treasure my whole life."

"Honestly, I don't think I've ever met so many people who just *get* me," I say. "I love that we can nerd out about this stuff. I love that we can tease Lena about the griffin bones but also be jittering with excitement because we might find them, too."

Lena tosses a pebble at my leg. "Hey. I don't know why you want to tease me about them. They are exciting! And there are so many fascinating things about their ties to the ancients. How many people can say that they were so close to mythical creatures?"

"And bonded as they looked for them? Probably nobody in the past hundred years!" Lauren says.

"Well, I'm thankful you all were here this year," Ella says. "It gave me the courage to sign up for some archaeology classes for next semester. And it gave me a lot of perspective seeing women who are actual adults, besides my family of course, who are having big, fulfilling experiences. And you didn't have to do anything crazy to have them."

"I suddenly feel old," I say, reminiscing about how my gray hairs used to bother me. It wasn't that long ago. And now, I don't even think about them. It's like something was unlocked. Like I have a bigger purpose, and that's not so important anymore.

"You're not old," Ella laughs, "But definitely wise. I appreciate all of you." We pause to grab her hands, pat her arm, and generally do that girl thing where you're like, "Aw, group hug," without the actual group hug. I feel my heart swell with love and companionship.

"We're certainly in a different spot from where we were last year," Lauren nudges me. "Now we're wise and have an amazing network of support."

"You keep talking about how things were tough last year ..." Alessia says. She's been quiet this whole time, and I know the gears are turning. That's just how she seems to operate. Quiet, but thinking.

I look at Lauren, not sure if we're ready to discuss last year ... and Thomas.

"It's a funny story." Lauren gives me a serious look, and I nod. I think we've all bonded enough. They can hear this one.

"OK." I take a deep breath. I hate reliving this moment. I had to several times when it first happened because, of course, I had to tell everyone. I couldn't just post on social media and crawl into a hole. I had to explain to my mom, and then my dad, and then my brother, who told Sarah, which was helpful, and Grandma Claudia, twice, because she couldn't believe it the first time. And some of my other family members, and Miranda, and some of my friends from outside of work because I definitely wasn't going to explain this to anyone else at work. We just aren't that close.

I am trying to fix that a bit, talking to other people at work. But anyway ...

I exhale. And then I launch into the story. "I got engaged to Thomas in August last year, and in late October, I needed to have a prong fixed on my engagement ring. So, I took it to the store where he bought it, and they called a couple days later so I could pick it up. I showed up at the store after work, and Lauren was there picking out a present for her sister."

"Right," Lauren continues. "I was at a client's home nearby doing a fitting for her wedding dress— they were having a November wedding, and it was the last one for the bride and bridesmaids—so I popped in the store to see if they had anything Taylor, my sister, would like."

"While I waited on the sales associate to get my ring, I was looking in the jewelry cases and happened to notice Lauren's engagement ring—it was an emerald cut diamond with two smaller triangular diamonds on either side, so not very common. I mentioned that my engagement ring was exactly like Lauren's, so we started talking about our wedding plans. Thomas and I were doing an October wedding the following year, which would have been a couple months ago, actually. Lauren and her fiancé were looking at a longer engagement because they wanted to live together first, and he was handling a lot of travel for work."

"So, we talked about colors and things we wanted at our weddings."

"And that's when the sales associate comes back with my ring. I'm thinking, 'Too funny that we have the same ring, right?' I get the ring, put it on. And then the sales associate asks, 'Is Thomas Everhart the name on the account?'"

"And that's when I started seeing colors swirling in front of my eyes," Lauren laughs.

I don't know *how* she can laugh at this point because I'm definitely not ready to laugh about it. In fact, at the time, when I saw the look on her face, I had a million thoughts flashing through my head. Clearly, she knew him or someone with the same name. Was he a murderer? I remember my stomach starting to churn as I saw Lauren's mouth drop open.

"Wait, what made you see colors?" Ella asks.

"Because that was my fiancé's name too." Lauren throws her hands apart in "ta-da" arms, and I confirm with a sober nod.

"Not just the same name. The same damn guy."

During the moment's pause, Alessia, Ella, and Lena all look at each other with wide eyes.

"So, you're saying you were engaged to the same man?" Lena offers.

"Yep," I say. "So, in the store, Lauren finally says, 'Did you say Thomas Everhart?' and I'm like, 'Yes. Do you know him?' and she says, 'That's my fiancé's name too.'"

Lauren jumps in. "We stared at each other for a full minute without saying anything, and the sales associate was standing calmly by the computer waiting for us to figure things out. Finally, she says, 'How funny! Does your fiancé live around here honey?' And I managed to stammer out that he does. Then I said he works at Pittsburgh Health Network as an actuary. The look on Kenzi's face told me everything. I knew it was the same guy."

I guess actuaries like to take risks and not just calculate them ...

As we told the story, I drifted back in my mind to that time. I was a different Kenzi. I could still feel the shock, the way the blood froze in my veins, and the words evaporated from my tongue. A heavy blanket of anger, regret, and self-doubt wrapped itself around me like a cocoon.

I really felt like time stood still for a moment as I grappled with that information. *My* Thomas was engaged to someone else *at the same time.* Lauren looked sick, and I'm sure my face was just as green. Or red. It's really hard to tell. I felt my eyes welling up and my breath coming in short bursts. Lauren was the one who seemed to pull herself together first. She wiped her eyes with the back of her hand and said, "I take it you had no idea." Clearly. I bit my lip and shook my head. How would I know? How did he do this? Better yet, why? What the hell?!

"I'll just punch this in and charge his account," the sales associate had said. "Maybe you girls should go talk somewhere private. I'm sure you could both use a friend right now, and no one knows better what you're going through than each other."

I nodded. The woman looked gravely at both of us and shook her head. "Men."

"Wanna grab a bite to eat?" Lauren had said.

"Um, I guess?" I had yet to calm the screaming voices in my head that were telling me that I should have seen a red flag somewhere and that people always walk all over me and how could I be so stupid. Lauren seemed like a calming presence despite having the exact same upset as me moments ago, so it wasn't a ridiculous idea to go off with a stranger to get food.

We walked down the street in silence as the shock set in. It was a brisk evening, with the sun having already set and a breeze rushing the fallen leaves past our feet. I wore my long mushroom leather jacket that I bought when I finished my first project at Baker & Willow, and I remember listening to the soothing swish swish as it rubbed past my dress pants. My breath shaky, my hands in the pockets, I rubbed my thumb across the band of my engagement ring, wondering when it all happened, what went wrong, and why.

Always the why. Like there should be an answer! Maybe he was just nuts. Or had brain damage. Or was, sorry IS, a narcissist. Maybe it wasn't me.

Maybe it was. Maybe I was someone to be taken advantage of. Maybe I was dirt to him.

Did he ever really love me?

"Kelli's has the best pizza in the South Hills of Pittsburgh," Lauren said softly.

"I've never eaten here before." Then I had that little panic that always rises whenever I have to eat out and don't plan ahead. "I—"

"They actually have an amazing cauliflower crust here," she said. "I always get it with the Margherita toppings."

"Funny you should say that …" I smile wanly. "That's the same thing I always get. I'm celiac, so I always do cauliflower crust."

Lauren chuckled and sniffed. Then she dug in her purse for a tissue. "I think this is exactly what we need then."

The details, as we traded them over a cauliflower crust pizza with Margherita toppings, went something like this.

- Lauren and Thomas met three years before that night, approximately, at a party because mutual friends invited them. They continued to connect through that group off and on for a couple years till they found that they were always off together talking.
- Thomas and I started dating about three months before he and Lauren were official, which is why he took me to the Christmas activities with his family.
- They officially started dating around Christmas last year and got engaged in June.
- This also explains why Thomas didn't have any social media.
- We got engaged in August.

- And Lauren and I met in October ... You know how that went.

By the end of dinner, we had both cried innumerable times, so our eyes were red, along with our noses—paper napkins aren't great for nose wiping.

"I don't know how we should tell him we know." Lauren said. "I want him to feel like we do. I almost want to turn this into a game."

"I want to go Carrie Underwood on his ass," I said. I was definitely switching over from upset about my life being ruined to revenge plot at that point, and I had a serious urge to dig "my key into the side of his pretty little souped-up" ... well, he had a Volkswagen Jetta, so not super fancy or anything, but he did like his car. He wasn't good enough for me to go to jail for though.

"Saving a little trouble for the next girl, huh?" Lauren said. "Personally, I'd like to drive his ass over a cliff." We both laughed the painful laugh of the duped. "Actually, I wonder if there is a healthy way to do this."

"I don't think this deserves a healthy approach," I said.

"Agreed. This is something where we should just do shots of tequila and show up on his doorstep together." Lauren pulled out her phone. "Oh, here's an article that says we should schedule a time to chat and let him know what we know. It says 'you' like there is only one person doing it though. Not both of us. I don't like that. I want shock."

"Totally."

"Hmmm." Lauren was reading something on her phone. "Yeah, this one says that you should talk about how his alibi doesn't add up and present evidence and let him feel safe enough to confess."

"Not feeling that one either."

"Nope. So should we humiliate him in public or let this happen at his apartment?"

I started shaking, thinking about how everyone would think I'm an idiot if we did it in public.

"I have an idea. Oh! You don't look OK. I promise this will be good. I want his friends to know what he's done, so what if we meet up with him next Friday night at Steel Pints in the Strip. We were talking about going there for his birthday."

"I could invite all our friends and tell them it is a surprise, so they don't tell Thomas."

"And I'll do the same. I get the feeling that he has a couple different friend groups since we both met friends and never met each other."

"What a creep." Then I swallowed hard. "I don't know how I can look at all those people and do this. I don't want them to think I'm stupid or that I deserved this." I started crying again, which should mean that I'm OK with looking like an idiot in public, but really, it never gets any easier.

"They won't think you're an idiot. You're the victim. And me. And it's not the victim's fault. We saw Thomas as the best he could be ... and he just *wasn't*. It's not our fault he played us."

"OK," I moaned.

"I wonder, though, how he thought he was going to marry us both. Kinda hard to pull that off, what with the whole living together thing. And the wedding license."

"That's true."

"I'm glad we figured it out now before we had our weddings completely planned."

"You're right." I wiped my nose on the napkin again and tried to look at the very tiny bright side to this evening's discovery.

Suddenly, Lauren started bawling. She waved her hands like she didn't know what to do. "I had the most beautiful dress sketched for the wedding. It had a sweetheart neckline with a mermaid skirt and a lace overlay ..." Her voice caught as she saw the dress falling to pieces in her mind. "I'm a wedding dress designer."

I sobbed out loud too because *I* could see the dress and see Lauren in it. Probably a beautiful cream with her long red hair and a bouquet of lilies. Now *I* was thinking about *her* wedding to *my* fiancé and crying over the fact that it wouldn't happen! "It sounds so beautiful!" I wailed.

"Can I get you ladies something?" Our server approached us with a look of concern. She put the tray she was carrying on her hip and put her free hand on the other one. Her name tag said "Kelli," and I realized she was the owner. She probably didn't need our bullshit in there that night.

I said, "Just the check" as Lauren said, "Do you have rum runners?" And then we both started cry-laughing.

Kelli sighed and scooted onto the bench beside Lauren. "Girls, what happened? And who is the asshole that did it?" We briefed her on our pain and appreciated the look of shock followed by absolutely murderous narrowing of her eyes. "I don't have rum runners, but I'm bringing you each a rum and Coke on the house. That scumbag. What an awful way to treat people! I'd throw all his stuff out in the street and take out a billboard to let everyone know what happened. I'll be right back with those drinks!" With that, Kelli jumped up and strode to the bar. We saw her pointing at us, and the bartender just shook his head. He saluted us and grabbed two drink glasses.

"A billboard! Now that's an idea." Lauren said.

"I can't imagine that's legal. Sounds like a defamation lawsuit if I've ever heard one."

The drinks arrived, and we continued to talk about all the ridiculous things that we would never actually do because, for one, I couldn't possibly do something that would hurt another person, and I also got that Lauren couldn't either ... but it was maybe a little healing to fantasize.

As we left Kelli's, I knew I needed to walk off the rum—that's one of the downsides to cauliflower crust, nothing to absorb the alcohol. I looked in the window of the shop next door, Merilee's Healing Magik, and found myself staring at crystals and books and little sachets of something that looked like tea. It was pretty, and I could see jewelry racks inside, so I agreed immediately when Lauren suggested we go in. I could use some "healing magik" anyway, I imagined.

A perky woman with a short brown bob and wearing a pretty floral kimono greeted us from the cashier's station. "Welcome! Are you here for the palm readings? Kim has an opening in about 20 minutes."

Lauren and I looked at each other. "I don't think I want to tempt fate right now," I muttered.

"We're good. Just looking." Lauren approached a table with little wooden bowls of rocks. Special rocks, apparently, because they were shiny and had cards that said what they were for, like "Chakra balancing," "Relationships"—dodging that one— "Physical ailments," etc.

"Sure! Let me know if you need any help!" The woman turned to a display and started adding more necklaces and bracelets from a box.

I wandered through the store. Lots of pretty stuff! Some fun shirts with "high vibe" sayings ... decks of tarot cards ... books on spells and—wait a second. That could be fun. I grabbed a book and searched for "revenge." Nope. I guess I need a black magic shop.

"What did you find?" Lauren asked. She tipped the cover to read the title on the spell book. "Oh ..." She chuckled. "Is there one to make his ding dong shrivel up and fall off?"

I snort-laughed and flipped through the index. "Sorry. No."

The woman from the desk was adding bundles of herbs to a display near us and must have heard at least part of the conversation. "Are you guys looking for a spell for something specific? Or just having fun? All good either way!" She appeared to notice our smeared eye makeup and probably could have guessed the story had something to do with a guy.

We looked at each other, and Lauren decided to spill the beans. "We just found out that we are engaged to the same man. Annnnnnd we thought there was something appropriate in here to, um, let him know how upset we are."

The woman frowned. "Wow. That's just awful." She put her hand on her hip and gazed off like she was thinking. "First of all, thank you for sharing that. I know you're both hurting, and it's still pretty fresh. I think I have something a little more productive than, uh, making his dick fall off ..." She wandered to the sachets of tea or herbs or whatever they are. "Try this."

I took the little beige mesh bag she offered and stared at the contents. It was filled with what looked like potpourri. "Do I put this in my tea?"

"No. It's a mix of herbs that will bounce bad karma back to its owner!" She handed another one to Lauren. We gave her an equally confused look. "You're familiar with karma, right?"

"Yes! So bad energy rewards bad energy, in this case." Lauren smelled the bag and made a face like it wasn't too bad.

"Exactly. And good energy rewards good energy. That's more what we're going for here." The woman gestured to the display. "As you can see, we don't have any revenge spells or anything else like that, so you want to work with something that will protect your energy and create like a bubble, so his bad energy just bounces off."

"Ah. I kind of want to make him hurt though ..." I was being honest. She seemed like the kind of person you could open up to.

The woman smiled. "Of course you do. This keeps his bad energy from coming to you and bounces it back to him. Trust me, he'll get what's coming, and you keep your hands clean. Will that work for you?"

"You know, I think it will," Lauren said. "Anything else you can recommend?"

The woman walked back to the cashier station. "I actually just put these out. These are apatite." She picked up two bracelets with blue-green beads and a silver charm. "This stone is good for clearing up our baggage and floating away the feelings around it. It reduces heaviness and anxiety and boosts our happy thoughts. Perfect for what you're going through. It can help you settle into the new you without all the bad feelings around what just happened. The lotus charm symbolizes hope and rebirth, strength and resilience. So really, this is the perfect pairing."

"OK, we'll take two." I reached for my wallet.

"Sounds good. I'm *giving* you the sachets, though. That's where a lot of the power is for protection. My gift."

We walked out of the store with our new magical bracelets and *spells* (the sachets) feeling slightly better than before. And the rum was wearing off, so that was ideal.

The entire week between that night and the Big Dump—which also seemed to be what my life had become—I had to work to blow Thomas off. Texting a bit, dodging his phone calls. I said I had a huge assignment dropped on me at work, so I would be doing overtime. Plus, I was designing a playhouse for my nieces and nephews, which wasn't a total lie, but it didn't take that much time either.

Lauren and I spent a lot of time on the phone with each other, crying, trying to make each other laugh, and generally being supportive. We tended to balance each other out, so it was a seesaw of emotions.

Then, it was finally time for the Big Dump. I walked into Steel Pints not knowing what to expect. Lauren said she was going to have Thomas meet her there. She couldn't bear to speak to him, let alone let him pick her up or hold hands with him as they walked in. I was in the same predicament.

The dread I wore like a cloak around my shoulders wrapped securely around my neck and chest, keeping my breathing shallow. For the entire period between meeting Lauren and that night, I felt like I was a shadow of myself. I barely ate. I certainly didn't dress like I normally would have. Everything was very black and white, and not just because I wear a lot of black and white. The breakup that was about to happen had already drained the songs from my head, the joy from my heart, and the color from my world. All I had left was the hope that things would eventually be OK. I knew they would be, but God this sucked.

As I walked into the bar, I wrapped my right fingers around the bracelet on my left hand. Hope, rebirth, ditching baggage. Here we come.

I spotted Lauren at a table with a couple other women in a back corner. She had a gold clip in her hair and wore a sage green sweater dress with leggings and boots. Thomas stood at the end of another table, still in his coat, on the opposite end of the restaurant. He must have just walked in.

I recognized about half the people at Thomas's table, so the others must have been his and Lauren's mutual friends.

Lauren glanced at me and then at Thomas. Her smile took on a strained quality. I swallowed, my heart throbbing in my throat, and met her halfway, the two of us walking together to where Thomas was standing.

By the time I got there, I felt like I was floating, like the scene wasn't real. The words in my throat felt like they came from someone else. Like I was on autopilot. Like I was watching my life crumble without having any control over it.

"Hi, honey," I said. I placed a hand on his arm.

He jumped a mile and nearly tripped trying to get away from my touch. I bet he was starting to piece things together, spotted that something was off, as he stood there looking at his two friend groups sitting together. We had walked up before he could really react to what was about to happen.

I clasped my hands and watched as he stared open-mouthed at me and then at Lauren.

"Hey, she made it!" Jason called from the end of the table. He was one of "our" friends, so he was about to get a shock by meeting Lauren.

I looked at Lauren. She was standing with her arms crossed, an unamused look on her face. "Don't even try to explain this, Thomas," she said. Her green eyes flashed, and I'm fairly certain she sent laser beams at him.

To his credit, he closed his mouth and didn't try to explain. Regaining his composure, Thomas approached the end of the table and held his hands in front of him like he was giving a speech to "all of you." "Friends, I'll be back in just a moment. It looks like there was some confusion about the party."

"No," I found myself saying. "The confusion wasn't about the party. There's some confusion about our relationship. And your relationship with Lauren."

The table went deathly silent then as all our friends strained to hear over the din of the bar. I glanced at the bewildered faces around me. Their friends and our friends looked back and forth like someone maybe knew something they didn't, but the funny thing was that it was just the three of us at the end of the table who knew the full story.

Lauren grabbed Thomas's arm so he couldn't leave. "Maybe you'd like to introduce your fiancé?" About half the table gasped. "Or maybe you'd like to introduce your other fiancé?" She gestured at me. I waved and smirked at him. She quickly explained to everyone how we met, and Thomas, turning whiter by the moment, knew the gig was up.

The amount of people making surprised "oh my God" faces at the table was 100%.

"What the hell is wrong with you, man?" Jason said. Thank you, Jason. That's exactly what I was thinking for the past week!

"Clearly, I'm not welcome here anymore. I'll just be going." Thomas turned and shuffled toward the door like he didn't even care.

For some reason, my feet decided to chase after him. I was disgusted, annoyed by his ambivalence, and beyond angry. "You're not going to apologize or say anything to us? Why would you think it's OK to do this to two people?"

Thomas shook his head and looked at me like he pitied me. "Kenzi, you just didn't get me. This is really on you."

I can't even explain the feelings that raced through my body after that. Was he dead inside? Did he think he could blame this on me?

"Cheater!" Lauren yelled across the bar. "Asshole!" Jason followed up. Again, thanks Jason!

Thomas waved them away and walked out the door. I dropped to my knees, crying. It didn't matter that I had on a new dress, black with white and purple flowers, and cute booties. Lauren and a girl in a denim jacket grabbed me, helped me up, and practically carried me to the table.

Denim-jacket girl, who I later learned was Shannon, wrapped her arms around both of us. "You guys don't deserve this. Come back and grab some dinner with us at least. We should celebrate something tonight, so it might as well be a new beginning for you both."

That weekend, Thomas texted to pick up his things, which I didn't actually throw out in the street like Kelli, the pizza place owner, suggested. I told him there would be a box on the doormat. I planned on just watching TV and ignoring him when he popped over, but I heard him outside the door and suddenly felt venomous.

I flung the door open. "How does someone even do this?" I said. I was fuming. Just seeing him infuriated me. It was like putting my hand on a hot stove. There was no other way to react.

And he didn't say a word. I could feel him staring at the wall calmly, like my existence didn't even faze him. What kind of person ...

"I guess I'm nothing but a toy to you," I said.

Still nothing. He didn't deny it. Maybe some people never got away from seeing people as pawns in their game of life.

"Clearly we're done, Kenzi," Thomas finally said. "Why keep talking about it?"

He was so cool when he spoke. Like nothing I said could stir his soul. Does he even have one?

Not long after that day, my duplex was ready. I signed the papers on my own. It would be mine alone. We had planned on buying it together, moving in together, but I wondered how he would have blown me off for that. Or if he would have moved in and just had a lot of late nights working or out of town meetings? Or moved Lauren into the other half and just run back and forth to his two wives? How does someone keep up a double life? It must be exhausting!

I drove through Chestnut Acres with the U-Haul to unload my stuff. Declan was there and a smattering of Thomas's and my old friends. I could tell they felt sorry for me, and it crushed me seeing them there. We didn't stay in touch long after that. I had the duplex to paint and wanted to unpack my stuff ... and the other side was empty, so I had to figure that out.

Lauren and I kept talking and supporting each other. We met up for coffee or dinner or shopping for things for the house once or twice a week and found that we had a lot more in common than a crappy ex. When Lauren mentioned that she was looking for a new apartment in the Southpointe area, I offered her the right half of the duplex to rent. We were starting to feel like sisters, and then we were neighbors too! I guess good things can come from really shitty things.

Speaking of ... we found out a few months after the Big Dump that Thomas was hospitalized with COVID a short time after the last time we spoke. He had it rough. And I don't know that he ever recovered his sense of taste, which feels a lot like karma considering how tasteless his behavior was.

Lauren seemed to bounce back and became even more outgoing and career-focused after the Big Dump, which is interesting considering she works in the wedding industry. I felt like I was floundering, though, just getting to work and getting through what I needed to. Miranda noticed, of course, and was very supportive. She gave me a lot of grace as well as some older sister-like wisdom as I trudged uphill.

This grief carried over into every part of my life! I still have trouble trusting others. And I've been quieter. I keep to myself more. It really broke me down. On the upside, I've busted through a lot of TV series that I had planned to watch that Thomas didn't want to watch, so ha! I read a lot of books, started learning Italian ... we all know how that went, *verdad*? Sorry, in Italian, *vero* (true)?

But the truth is ... I stopped dreaming about a big life. I started thinking about escaping. Moving away—

If it's not perfect, why bother?

Maybe I took all the responsibility for the failure of this relationship. He certainly tried to push it off on me.

Maybe there is some deeper truth in my scars.

Chapter 12

The next morning, I can hear shouting on the veranda as all the diggers meander to the dining room for a breakfast of quiches and fresh fruit. Everyone looks at each other uncomfortably. It's Ella and Edo ... again. After two-and-a-half weeks, we are all used to it but still don't know how to react.

Gianmarco comes down the stairs a moment later, mutters something I don't understand, and exits onto the porch. From the tone of his voice and the fact that he points at the road, I know he is telling Edoardo to leave. A moment later, he does, and then I see Gianmarco speaking sternly to Ella, who looks like she wants to cry.

As eating and talking resume, father and daughter slip into the dining room and find seats at the table. Ottavia, wrapped in a muted rainbow knit shawl with a stylish broach, sips an espresso at the end of the table. She bends her head low to whisper with Gianmarco. I glance at Ella beside me and see that her face is pink. But she doesn't look upset or defiant. She looks ... calm. Vibrant. I hope she's OK.

I reach over and pat her arm. When she looks at me, I give her a tight I've-been-there smile. She nods and discreetly wipes her eye.

"I did it." Ella still has that air of calm about her like the aftermath of a tornado. Her big brown eyes are wide with the realization. I'm not totally sure what she means, but I could guess. But I shouldn't guess.

"Did what?" I whisper.

"I broke up with Edo." She shakes a bit as she breathes in deeply. Then she exhales a thousand stresses into the air. They flutter to the window like butterflies and vanish.

My phone vibrates for a text in my pocket, but I ignore it. "I guess he didn't take it well."

"I'll spare you the details. He wasn't happy, but he's not my problem anymore." She sips her hot tea and looks pensive. "I was thinking about the story you told me last night, about Thomas, your ex, and how he played you, and I thought that if I knew something wasn't right, why would I waste my time? You didn't have control over what happened to you. I do. So, I decided to ... 'Seize the day'? Is that the phrase?"

I chuckle. "Yes, that's the phrase. Wow. I'm ... shocked? Proud of you for sure." I tear up and bite my lip. I can't believe someone learned from my story. My horrible, horrible story. About my broken past. Maybe it serves a purpose after all. I always wondered why it had to happen to me. But if it helps save someone from stretching out a crappy relationship ... Then I start crying for real. I throw my arms around Ella and hug her tight. "It's amazing," I whisper into her hair.

By this point, everyone at the table is watching us. As I pull away from Ella, I see that Lauren has tears in her eyes too. She probably overheard what we were saying. Plus, tears are just contagious. She pats me on the back. "You OK?" And she nods at Ella. "Ella?"

"Better than OK," I say through a teary smile. Then I wipe my eyes and turn back to my meal.

Ella sniffs and then laughs. "It feels weird to think that I don't need to have all the answers and have my future all planned out and keep worrying that Edo will think I'm cheating on him. This is going to be one hell of a Christmas."

It's inspiring to see Ella stand up for herself and set that boundary. I glance at my phone and realize that maybe I need to set some boundaries too.

Hon, did you ask everyone what their favorite dish is? It might be nice if each person has something that they really like. That way, everyone is happy.

Dear Lord, Mom. This reminds me of the time that Mom was in charge of her team's ad campaigns at work AND the holiday luncheon. At the same time. And she was sooooo busy asking everyone what to do ...

"So, I have Sammy's, Lawson's, and Sandwich Hut delivering at 11." Mom was in the living room on the phone, crossing her legs, then uncrossing, shifting, crossing. I had learned from watching her over the years that this was one of her signature uncomfortable moves. She paused. She frowned. "Well, I asked what everyone wanted." Another frown. "I thought it would be nice if everyone was happy." A sigh. "Well, I'll know for next time. But I did keep to the budget." Her voice suddenly got high and defensive. "I think it's fine to have a lasagna and sandwiches. We have salad too."

I was doing homework at the dining room table, and she approached me a moment after hanging up. "I think it's fine to have variety, but no one is happy with my choices. Which is funny because I made those choices to keep everyone happy. They are depending on me to make this luncheon wonderful." She put her hands on her hips. Mom's hair was longer and blonder then, sweeping her shoulder blades in the back as she turned to pace the room. She still wore her gray dress slacks and a floral blouse from work, but she was barefoot.

"Don't worry about it, Mom. I'm sure you are doing great. If they don't appreciate it, then don't volunteer next time." Declan was reading a novel *for his English class on the couch, legs draped over the arm, a thick pillow under his head.*

"No one else volunteers, so I have to do it."

"Do you ever wonder what would happen if you just didn't volunteer though? What if you allowed someone else to step up? What if someone else was just waiting for the opportunity to organize the luncheon and they think that they can't because you love doing it?"

"I do love doing it."

"But your boss always complains. Why would you love it?"

"I don't know, Declan." Mom sounded sour. She sat down at the kitchen table and began writing Christmas cards.

"I thought you already sent out cards," I said.

"These are for the retirement home beside my work." Mom licked the envelope and pressed it shut. "A group of us are handling cards for them because some of the residents don't have any family."

"Mom, you should rest too." Declan shut his book and started writing in his notebook.

"I do rest." She continued writing cards. "Those poor people. I hope I'm not like that when I'm older. I want my family to visit me."

"When Kenzi is done with her homework, we could make hot chocolate and watch a movie," Declan suggested.

"Or you kids can help me with these cards. Think of those poor old people."

I'm pretty sure I strained an eye rolling it so hard. "For real Mom."

"Nothing makes us happier than helping others be happy."

The phone rang, and Declan answered. "Yeah, I'll be right there." He hung up. "That was Lawson's. One of the cooks called in sick, so I'm going to pick up an extra shift."

"Go ahead. Kenzi can help me."

I remember that night we ended up making cards, baking cookies, and checking on our neighbor whose husband had just passed. By the time we got home, I had to shower quickly and go to bed. So much for enjoying myself. That must be where I got it ...

———

As I walk to the dig site, I keep looking at the home screen with the text notification. On and off. On and off.

Did you ask everyone what their favorite dish is?

Did you ask everyone what their favorite dish is?

Did you ask everyone what their favorite dish is?

"Ella, I'm really happy for you," Lauren was saying. "*You* teach people how to treat you. This is a step in the direction of people treating you the way you're supposed to be treated. You are kind and fun to hang out with. And you're serious about your studies. You'll go far someday, I'm sure of it."

"Wha-? What did you say?" I stammer.

"You want me to repeat the compliment?"

"I don't mind," Ella says. "Say it again. A little louder!" She laughs and waves her hands to encourage Lauren.

"I mean the first part." I am starting to put pieces together.

"You teach people how to treat you?"

"That." Oh my God.

"By the way, I was thinking of ordering some desserts from The Church Ladies for my family's Christmas." Lauren sets her trowel down and presses her hands together to stretch her wrists.

"What church ladies?" I ask.

"Have you met Bev Walker?" Lauren says. "Actually, I don't know her last name, but she's always out walking her dog, this gorgeous Airedale terrier named 'Luna,' so I just think of her as 'Bev the walker': Bev Walker."

"I don't know her. I'm not home during the day."

"Right. Sometimes when I'm on the porch, she stops to talk. But she and some of the other ladies from her church started a dessert business called ... The Church Ladies." Lauren makes ta-da hands. "She dropped off some cookies one time, and they were amazing. Little chocolate drop cookies. So good."

"Funny, I don't remember trying those."

"They were that good. I ate them all before you got home." Lauren does her best to look embarrassed, but she's so *not* embarrassed about not sharing the cookies. Boo.

"Some bestie you are!" I make a sour face at her.

248

"Anyway ... I was going to order some cookies from them for my family's Christmas gathering. Want to order stuff for your crew too? It would lighten the load for sure."

I raise my eyebrows. Definitely down with working smarter, not harder. "Yes. Is there a menu?"

"I have their website. Bev's niece designed it for them. It's super cute."

See? I can do this. I can plan ahead and get all the stuff I need.

———

The mermaid in all her glory has been exposed. She's a little dirty, but you can see the distinct shape of her beige body, her green tail, her brown hair ... she's striking. I'm always amazed by art from thousands of years ago. How detailed it was. It's not perfect, but wow, that mermaid is something special. I can't believe I was here to see her unveiled.

A few clouds flit across the sky today. When we describe them, Julie refers to them as "mare's tails," which I think means they are cirrus. Really pretty and wispy. It means that the sun dapples the ground around the dig and lights the tent spectacularly one moment and then dances away the next. It sort of keeps me from lulling into a mindless digging motion, which is good, but it also means I feel a bit restless.

With only a couple days left, I find myself wondering what life will be like afterward. Will I miss this? And the people? Will I feel the same kind of magic when I come back to help with the event center? Will I do a dig again? Do I want to? I sigh. The day is just perfect and stressless, and I haven't felt like this in a long time. Maybe I don't need to feel so caught up in needing to take care of everyone and everything. I haven't replied to my mom yet, which I will, but I'm not ready. And she actually hasn't called to see if I've been kidnapped and forced into slavery making ravioli yet, so that's a good sign.

I feel almost carefree. It's weird.

Nearby, I notice that Julie's group has gathered around her and is peering at the ground. Her face is lit up with joy. Soon, I see her lift something small between her finger and thumb. She raises a tiny brush to it and hands it to one of her dig partners.

By now, my whole group is watching. Lena hops over to see what it is and motions for the rest of us.

"It feels like a ring," Julie is saying. "What does it look like?"

Lena rinses it with her water bottle and holds it so all of us can see. "It's Venus. Oh my! And there is a dove on her shoulder. It looks like it has a note in its beak." She wipes it a bit. "It's a love letter. This is a common symbol for a secret love or for someone believing that true love will find them."

She turns the ring in her hand and rubs the inside of the band. "It's engraved too. Look!"

Each of us gets a turn to peer at the little ring with its creamy white stone, the chiseled image of Venus on its face. Inside the band, I can clearly make out the engraving, DOMITIA LONGINA." Our empress believed in true love.

I snap a picture of the ring and text it to my mom with a description of what Lena said. Then I tell her I already have the menu planned and it will be great. No sweat. Confidence. Right?

———

The next afternoon, I decide to take a break from the dig to walk around the property. Mom never responded to my text, and now I'm getting anxious. I think I pissed her off.

But maybe she needed it, right? I didn't do it on purpose. I was just trying to be firm and let her know that I have a handle on things. She can relax, you know? It's important for her to be able to delegate and not keep checking in on the people she hands stuff off to. She needs to trust me. She asked me to do it, and it's a big job, but I've got it.

I've got it, right?

Right. I do. I need to stop doubting myself. What is it that Jennifer Halliday says? *When we second guess ourselves, we are saying that we can't trust ourselves to do a job to the best of our ability.* And that's just silly! Why would I do something in any way but to the best of my ability?

Unless I'm trying to get out of doing it in the future.

I snort-laugh aloud at this one. And then I realize that I'm no longer enjoying the breezy beautiful day and, instead, am ruminating on that text and Mom's lack of response while pacing through the rows of lemon trees like I'm tracking a serial killer. I'm sure Detective Kenzi looks ridiculous.

Maybe I've hurt my mom, and I really didn't want that. I pull out my phone to apologize and tell her we can talk about her ideas for the menu. Then I put it away again.

No, I'm not going to be an enabler to her people pleasing and need for control. I'm going to be strong.

I'll at least be strong till this evening. Because I can keep myself busy.

Is that reaaaaaally being strong? Or is that just keeping myself busy till I get the chance to break down and call her.

Gah. I hate this.

OK, Lauren would want me to be strong and set healthy boundaries. And I know that's the best thing to do. Also, she would suggest that I at least enjoy the freaking lemon trees while I'm here because we only have a couple days left, and isn't that why I said I wanted to wander off from the group anyway?

"You OK Kenzi?" Ella approaches me and puts her hands in the pockets of her black joggers.

"Of course!" I briefly explain what I'm thinking about. "I'm just trying to convince myself that I shouldn't say anything else and that it is the right thing to do."

"Does it help if I say that you shouldn't say anything else and that it is the right thing to do?" Ella laughs.

"Maybe." I playfully give her a sour look. "What's weird is that I understand why she does this, but I keep letting her do it."

"At least you know what's going on. Now you can make her stop doing that to you." Ella responds.

"Mmmmm." I join her in walking back to their porch, and we both sit on a glider.

"Lemons used to be so prized that royalty would give them as gifts to each other."

"Really?"

"And now, they are so common that you get a slice in every glass of water in every restaurant in the world, it seems."

"That's true. Funny how things change."

"Everything changes from one generation to the next. What matters is what we make of the changes. Your mom probably never knew that she was desperately trying to get people to like her. Why do you think she did that?"

"I'm not sure. She and my dad divorced when I was young, and she never dated till I was in high school. He was the one who said they should end it. Maybe she felt like no one could love her."

"That could be it. It could be something else too, since we don't know everything she went through, but it's likely that had something to do with it. And since she's remarried, she likely feels lovable now.

But that doesn't mean that she's healed the part of her that felt unlovable."

"Are you sure you're not a philosophy major, Ella?" I laugh.

She smiles. "I've been paying attention to what you and Lauren and the others are saying and just thinking a lot about the why behind everything. It's really opened my eyes having you all here. I have older brothers and my sister, but to watch people outside of my family and learn about them gives me a new perspective on my own problems."

"I bet it would." Just then, my phone buzzes, and I whip it out of my pocket so fast that I almost throw it from the momentum. I relax when I see that it's Declan. He's telling me about them shipping some of the kids' presents to my house, to arrive on December 23rd. I imagine a dump truck backing up and just unloading on my porch. "Why do you think we like to make holidays complicated? My brother has four kids, and he's been suggesting things for me to get them, *and* he and Sarah, his wife, have been ordering things to ship over. What are they going to do after Christmas? Ship all the presents back to Europe?"

"Wow, that is complicated. Maybe I won't have kids." She bugs her eyes, telling me that her 20-year-old brain has way better things to worry about than shipping toys back and forth halfway across the world.

I hear boot falls on the concrete porch and see Nico approaching with a basket of grapes from the small vineyard on site. *"Vuoi dell'uva?"*

"He asked if we would like some grapes," Ella says. Her cheeks glow as she turns back to him. *"Grazie! Ovviamente! Per favore unisciti a noi!"*

"Grazie," I reply. I stand and take a small bunch from the basket. "I should get back to the dig, though. You guys enjoy!" I manage to wink at Ella as Nico is sitting, so he doesn't notice me. She shoots me a look and turns to Nico.

"Ciao, Kenzi!" Ella says.

I peek at them as I round the corner and see Nico intensely listening to Ella. She laughs, and it ripples through the air. Nico drinks it in. I hope something sparks for those two.

My phone vibrates, and I glance at the screen. An email from Logan. A little tingle delights through my belly as I realize that I'm kind of excited to hear from him. It's been a few days. I immediately pop it open, shading the phone to try to read it in the bright sunlight.

Hi Kenzi,

A ruby? Amazing! Does anyone know the history? I'm curious if it belonged to the emperor and his family. It probably belongs to someone in the nobility. Let me know if you find anything out!

I poked around online and didn't find anything important, but since you have people there from the university, maybe they have some insight. I'd love to hear about it.

We had snow here this week, but it's back to brown and gray since it rained last night. Typical Pittsburgh holiday colors!

I snort-laugh because it's true. I can't believe I'm wearing a light jacket and walking in the sunshine right now. It hardly feels like December.

I'm looking forward to seeing you when you get back! I'm sure you have lots of stories and pictures from your time abroad.

Logan

Another little ripple. "Looking forward to seeing you." I shouldn't make it mean anything. Of course, he's looking forward to seeing me. I'm a curiosity right now. I did something really unusual. Who takes off for Italy and digs up relics for a month? Especially right before Christmas when it's not your profession.

When I get back to the dig site, I see the rest of the team scraping through the dirt, laughing, chatting, and looking at small rocks that don't mean anything, tossing them aside. Wow. I was a part of this. I feel like I'm having an out of body experience as I'm glancing around, admiring the mermaid mosaic on the wall ... but that weird chunk of missing wall in the upper left corner is bugging me. What's beyond it? Why isn't it filled with dirt?

"*Mi scuzi*, Dr. Rossi." I stroll over to him. I'm going to ask. The worst he can say is that he doesn't know. I'm here helping. He's here learning. We are a team. This is OK, Kenzi. It's OK to ask and be bold and *good grief!* I'm giving myself an internal pep talk.

What's new?

"Ah, Kenzi," he says with a smile. "Did you find something else?"

"No, I just had a couple questions. Is that OK?"

"Questions are always OK." He leans against the table and crosses his arms over his chest like he's ready to listen.

I forgot how much I like professors who love their work. "Do you know what's behind the far wall?" I point so he knows what I mean.

"You're curious about that hole too. I would have expected it to be filled in with dirt behind that wall ... We aren't sure yet, but we did get back the Lidar reports. It looks like a series of caves go back into the hillside there. One could abut the wall. It's definitely worth a deeper look, but I will need a team trained for exploring them to make sure they are safe, checking for supports and stability. We don't know if they are manmade or created by underground channels where water was rushing by. Do you understand what I mean?"

"That makes sense." I pause. "I would love to see back in there."

"I'll show you what we can see ... Come." Dr. Rossi leads me down into the dig site and across the tiled mermaid mosaic on the floor. He turns on his cell phone flashlight and shines it through the hole.

I raise up on my toes and see what looks like a hallway into the hillside. It stretches on past the glow of the flashlight. The cave is about the size of a doorway and sits directly behind the chink in the wall. "I wish I could go back and follow it."

"It's likely just a cave caused by groundwater. The map shows this one curving off to the right and ending near the lake, so I imagine there is a spring at the end where the water finally goes above ground and washes into the lake."

"That makes sense. It's less exciting than I imagined though." I laugh.

"Often, archaeology is. It isn't all Indiana Jones." Dr. Rossi chuckles and brushes some dirt from the design on the wall. "We will explore it eventually, but as I said, it's likely just a cave. No hidden treasure or anything special. Maybe some animal bones."

"You're probably right." Darn. "Did you learn anything new about the ruby?" Might as well ask since Logan mentioned it.

"Nothing new, but my graduate students are searching for articles this week. If they find anything, I'll report it."

"Is there a way we can stay in the loop after we leave? Tomorrow is our last day."

"True. I'll ask them to set up a Facebook group and post new findings in there."

"I like that idea! Thank you for showing me this and answering my questions."

"It's always wonderful to talk to people who are curious about the past. Please don't ever hesitate to ask questions. We love what we do and love talking about it."

"I'll keep that in mind."

Just then, my phone buzzes persistently. It's Mom. "Sorry, I have to take this." Dr. Rossi nods to me as I walk back to the edge of the site.

"Kenzi! I thought I would just call since it's hard to do the texting thing and know what we mean."

"OK ..." I'm a little confused. I guess the emojis aren't enough. Sometimes my mom is so funny!

"I know you said you have the menu handled, but I wasn't sure if Declan and Sarah approved it yet. You know it's tough with all the kids, and you want to make sure that they have things they like to eat. I want to make everyone happy!"

I feel like running. I just ... I thought I had this handled. It's OK. "The menu is done, Mom, but I can pull the list together and send a Google doc link to you and Declan. If there is something else that needs to be added, you guys can add it, but we have to be reasonable. There aren't that many of us, and no one wants to take home an entire buffet. I won't be able to fit a ton of extra food in my fridge, and I'm not throwing it out."

Breathe Kenzi. I hope that wasn't too stern. "Mom, I know you want it to be perfect, but you can't make everyone happy. That's not your job. We are having a great meal together—it will be excellent!—and that's what matters!" Where did that come from? Thank you, Jennifer Halliday! "I think everyone will enjoy what we have. Please stop worrying about it." I said that last bit so it sounded like a hug in my voice.

Wasn't there something I was supposed to add to the list though?

Mom was uncharacteristically quiet. "I think you're right Kenzi." I could hear her breathing on the other end. "Could you just check one thing for me? Make sure there is something special for Grandma Claudia." Mom was getting revved up again. "She likes boozy desserts. Like rum cake? No, that's a summer thing. Should I just call a local caterer and have them do it?"

"Mom, I appreciate your help. Can you add that to the document when I send you the link?"

"I suppose I can."

"I know you're trying to help, but this needs to stop. I'm on vacation, trying to do some good work, enjoying myself, and I need a break." Not sure how Mom is going to take all this, so I'm just going to keep going. "You need to trust me. You asked me to handle this. I can do this." I can? "I need you to know that not everything is going to be perfect, but I'll do the best I can. And it will be wonderful."

"I know you will, sweetie," Mom sounds a little choked up.

"I need to go. I love you."

"Love you too, baby."

Chapter 13

When I get to breakfast the next morning, day 20, our final dig day, I see the group of volunteers clustered around Dr. Rossi at the breakfast table. A huge white paper is stretched out, and he's pointing to something.

"Ah, Kenzi," he says, "this is what I was talking about yesterday. I had the Lidar results printed so I could show everyone."

The warmth of the crowd and heat from the kitchen, where Sabrina was probably making rolls this morning, based on the huge pile of them on the table, makes me a little too warm. I push up the sleeves of my emerald cotton shirt and lean on the table with the group.

"This is the cave system behind the cracked wall." Dr. Rossi traces it toward Lago Alba. "It ends here with this larger hollow area and likely opens into a stream that runs to the lake."

"This is a fascinating technology," Lena says.

"It really is," Dr. Rossi responds. He clears the paper from the table, and everyone moves toward their chairs.

Aside from the rolls (yes, she made a couple gluten-free for me!), we have hard-boiled eggs, bacon, some cheeses, and fruit. There is also *pangiallo*, an Italian Christmas "cake" made from dried fruits and nuts mixed with oil, wine, and flour. Thanks, Sabrina, for using almond flour! I lop off a chunk of goat cheese, because I can, and scoop up some eggs, fruit, bacon, and *pangiallo* from the trays as they are passed around. I'm really going to miss having someone cook for me!

"You know what I'm going to miss?" Lena says, her eyes a million miles away. I notice that Dr. Rossi is looking at her intently.

"Looking for griffins?" Alessia laughs.

"Looking for griffins." Lena sighs. "I still want to see one. And I don't know when I'll get to now."

Dr. Rossi looks like he's debating something, and then, he leans forward and puts his hands on the table. "Lena, there is a dig site north of Rome, and I'm heading there after Christmas. If you're interested, I could talk to your advisor and see about course credits if you want to join us. We can figure out the best way for you to continue your studies and do what you want. If you want." He grew quiet toward the end.

That was possibly the most adorable and nerdy offer I've ever heard.

"I would love that!" Lena said. "I was reading an article about a dig north of the city—I'm hoping it's the one you mentioned—and it said that there was a mosaic similar to the one at Piazza Armerina in Sicily, with the exotic animals being hunted. There is a griffin on the Sicilian mosaic. Is there one on the mosaic at your dig?"

"The mosaic is so big that we've only uncovered a bit of it yet: elephants, lions, and gazelles." Dr. Rossi gazes adoringly at Lena. "I would like to help you find your griffin if he's there."

I can practically feel the joy emanating from her as she throws her arms around Dr. Rossi. *"Perfetto!"* she says.

———

After an uneventful morning and our final perfect lunch at the villa, Lauren and I stop by the table of finds before returning to the dig site.

One of the grad students who came in with Dr. Rossi this morning is working on the pottery. Some of the pieces have been assembled, while most of them lay on the table, waiting to be tried. The student has separated the pieces into piles based on the presence of an image or the shade of terracotta, but they still have a difficult task looming ahead that will likely take months.

I definitely don't envy them, but I look forward to seeing their progress in our dig group online.

It seems like we have been here a lifetime now. The days before the dig are a blur as I think back to what it's like anywhere but here. I feel like this is my home. This is where I belong. This is where I was finally able to relax and discover, to rest and grow. It's been a crucible for change. And it's beautiful.

I pick up the ruby necklace from the table and another grad student looks up. I smile and just look at the necklace in my hands. The thickness of the chain likely kept it intact so we could examine it thousands of years after it was lost. I wonder if Domitia missed it. I wonder if her husband knew about it. I wonder if he's the one who took it.

I wonder how much she was hurting to be taken away from one husband—did she love her first husband?—and then marry another man who she didn't love ... and to fall in love with someone she could only be with in fleeting moments.

It's no wonder the whole of humanity is just hurting and hurting and hurting. We're built on pain. How much of this is embedded in our DNA? In what's around us? In the dirt?

It's strange to think that there are stories embedded in these objects, too, that we will never know. Stories buried with the teller rather than with the item itself.

And we can only dream of what they are.

I pull out my phone to take a picture of the necklace and fumble them both in my hands. The necklace lands on the table, which is covered with a rubbery tablecloth, likely for this very reason. I manage not to drop my phone, which is a miracle.

But as I pick up the necklace again, I realize that the back wasn't just a support for the gemstone, but rather, a compartment. It's flung open now, having hit just right—I feel like I should curtsy—revealing a pair of initials carved on the inside of the metal. It wasn't visible with the back closed. In block letters are "DL," something that might be an ampersand, and "MT." Domitia Longina and Marius Tatius.

"Lauren, I think we know who this belonged to now." I hold up the necklace so she can see the inside.

Lauren gasps and tips it up to see better. "It really is. I wonder if she was at least happy in her moments with Marius."

"I hope so." I see Dr. Rossi and gesture for him to come over. "Look at this!"

He takes the necklace from my hand and gazes at it. I think he's going to cry. Which is adorable. I love when people are doing work that matters to them. His eyes glassy, he just says, "Beautiful."

As Lauren and I wander back to the dig site and sit down with our friends, I see Lauren gazing off in the direction of Angelo. She reminded me of his name this morning when she was talking about him fondly, and it finally stuck in my head! She frowns.

"You good?" I ask.

"I should probably talk to Angelo before we leave," she says, a wistful look in her eye. "I like him, but ... the distance ... I don't know."

"Makes sense." I squeeze her hand in support. Then to the group, I add, "The ruby was definitely Domitia's," and tell them what I found.

"So, being clumsy actually panned out," Lauren laughs.

"I suppose it did!" Ha! So, I dropped something and broke it in a good way! Who knew that could possibly happen?

———

I brush the dirt from my hands and walk back to the villa with the others. We did it! I never in a million years would have thought that I would fly to Italy and dig around in the dirt for artifacts—let alone actually find some!—and hang out with such amazing people.

We did it.

Maybe this isn't a big thing for everyone, but it is for me. I never do new things because, hello, there is such a huge chance that I will do them wrong, and break stuff (which I did here), but it was OK because it was already broken. And honestly, it was OK overall. Really.

"Wow, that was amazing." Lauren gives me a little smile that says, "proud of us," and I return the smile. "This was a really cool experience. Glad you were by my side."

"Me too." I pause on the porch of the villa and hug her. Then we head upstairs for showers before dinner. I heard that there would be lasagna tonight, and my stomach is already rumbling at the thought. Yay!

We return to the table with wet hair because, hello, food, and I'm starving! Lauren and I find seats at the table, and I want to cry. These are my friends! I look around and see so many faces I will miss. I see Angelo and his eyebrows across the table. He's staring intently at Lauren. He's clearly got a thing for her, too. I wonder if they will try to make it work.

The lasagna is served, and Gianmarco stands with his glass of chianti. *"Amici, famiglia* ... I call you all the same because you have become like family to us over the past few weeks. We have been honored to share our home and our table with you. I am overjoyed by your generosity in coming to help us with this unique project, and I am also blessed beyond belief by what we have discovered here together.

"I don't speak of just the treasures that we have unearthed, but also of the stories that come with those treasures. Of the bonds that have been created between our many different volunteers. We come from many countries, but I believe that we have truly found a home here together this Christmas season.

"Every one of you is welcome at Villa Zangari any time you like. You are all my honored guests, and I am humbled to be now part of your *famiglia.* Blessings to you all, and safe travels in the morning. May your hearts find their way to Castel Gandolfo again in the future."

I'm not crying. *I'm not crying.* But then I make eye contact with Ella, and sure enough, I lose it. She feels like a little cousin at this point, and I don't think keeping up on social media will be enough.

And Lena, Alessia, and Julie. I want to see what Lena finds on her next dig and follow Julie on her next adventure! And hear about Alessia's third graders!

I put my hand on my heart and close my eyes to will the tears away. I hear a sob to my left and open my eyes to see that Alessia is hugging Lauren. Lena jumps up and throws her arms around both Lauren and me, and finally, my tears are in free-flow.

I feel like I've finally opened up to trusting and caring and *being* with those around me, and God, I'm going to miss this. I don't think I've ever walked into a place feeling so uncomfortable and left it feeling like it was the only place on the planet I truly belong.

But maybe I can bring that home with me.

"I'm going to miss you girls!" Lena says into my hair.

"Me too!" Lauren and I cry out together. Then we laugh.

The scene around the table has devolved into many pockets of hugs similar to ours. Which makes me want to cry even harder. Wow, humans, who knew I could care about so many of you so deeply!

It's much easier to imagine that most humans are horrible because they don't use their turn signal to change lanes.

Really getting to know people lets you move beyond that assumption. These people have passions and dreams. They have been about as real as real can get this month.

As real as dirt.

I would have happily died after the tiramisu we had that night. Boom, done. Best ending to a life that was often a dumpster-fire-cluster-fuck with a dead cat in it but was starting to feel more like just me. Just perfectly imperfect. And full of love and joy.

And I kinda miss my job too. Maybe I can find a little more of this there.

But instead of kicking the bucket, I actually waddle outside with Lauren and my very full stomach and decide that I want a little quiet time to just feel.

And then Angelo approaches. "Want to walk with me, Lauren?"

"Sure," she says. "Giorgio's?" He agrees, and the two of them head off toward the beach.

"I'll catch up in a bit," I call to Lauren. I should give them time to figure things out. They do look really sweet together, and I love seeing Lauren happy.

I walk through the lemon grove and down a path that winds behind the dig site. Over my shoulder, I see Lago Albano, the sun's rays playing on the surface of the indigo water, sending light sparkling off in every direction. Never will there be another moment like this.

I wander into the garden and look out over the wildflower patch at the lake. I snap a couple pictures for social. Then I breathe. Just breathe. And I feel like I should anchor into this moment forever. I push my loafers off, root my toes in the ground, and close my eyes. It feels important, necessary. It feels a bit ridiculous, but hey, I'm not going to judge what my gut tells me to do. Jennifer Halliday says I should trust my gut because it will lead me to great places.

Like Italy, where I can get amazing gluten-free lasagna and tiramisu. For my gut. Who knew it was so clever?

And in that moment of just breathing and enjoying the fullness of my happy belly, the scent of lemon and wildflowers and earth, hearing the wind in the trees ... I finally think I feel what Julie was talking about. The slightest vibration of the earth. I let out a happy sigh.

"You finally feel what I mean, Kenzi?" I nearly pee my pants. I'll blame too much wine for that. Julie is sitting on a bench about ten feet away, behind me a bit. I was so engrossed in the lake and the view that I didn't give my sanctuary a good look before shutting my eyes and using my other senses. Oops!

"Julie, this is amazing." I slowly approach the bench, shoes in hand.

"Have a seat. I'm enjoying the last evening here. You?"

"I am ... I'm going to miss it." I sit down and return to just breathing. "How did you know it was me?"

"I heard you sigh. It sounded like you ... but happier. Freer. I took a chance and assumed that you had finally discovered peace."

"I think I have." I close my eyes, and for a few minutes, we sit together in silence. Just us, the breeze, and the beauty surrounding us, pulsing slowly through our fingertips, our souls, and everything. I feel so connected to the world right now that I could cry.

Again.

In the silence, I feel the vibration repeating. It works its way through me. This must be what Julie was talking about!

"I feel it. I feel the vibration of the land and the plants and animals around us. Just like you said."

And then I feel a hard jolt that nearly knocks me off the bench. My eyes fly open. I grab the bench with one hand and Julie's hand with the other. The rumble continues for a moment, and then the area around us takes on an almost sickly quiet.

"You OK?" Julie says.

"Yeah. You?"

"I am." Julie clears her throat. She doesn't sound shaken, but she clearly is by her body language. I am too, so no judgment. "That was an earthquake, by the way. *Not* the ground vibrating under our feet. Totally different experience than that!"

I laugh nervously. "You're right."

"Shall we head back to the house and see how everyone is?"

"Let's do that." I stand and slip my loafers back on. "Hold my arm, just in case any cracks opened up anywhere."

"I was going to ask. I made it out here fine with my cane, but it's best to be safe!"

I walk back toward the house a changed woman. A bit nervous. Definitely literally shaken. The house looks fine. I don't think the quake was enough to really do damage. Not that I've ever been through an earthquake before, but this was a gentle rumble. I didn't even fall over.

We enter the house, and everyone is in the dining room, buzzing. I guess earthquakes are exciting for everyone!

Then Ella approaches me. "Where is Lauren?"

"She's walking to the beach with Angelo. I'm sure she's fine."

"Ah, that's good then. Angelo is a sweetheart."

"Good to know." I smile. I'm not like worried about her or about her being with Angelo. He doesn't give off any creepy vibes or anything. I just can't get over the eyebrows. What is my problem?

Just then, the kitchen door swings open.

"Lauren fell in a hole," Angelo yells. His face is red, and he looks panicked.

"Fell in a *hole*? Is she hurt?" And I'm wondering why the heck he didn't just help her back to the house. We've all stepped in a pothole before and turned our ankles. Or maybe that's just me.

"She said she's OK! But it's too deep. She can't climb out, and I can't reach her hand."

"Oh. Oh shit!" I have no idea what to do. I was thinking bitty hole, and it's more like a tank trap. Awesome.

"Do you need a ladder? A rope? What would work?" Gianmarco steps up.

"I don't know what's safe. The ground collapsed, and she fell in."

Now I get it. And, I've seen this sort of thing before. I jump into the convo. "It probably isn't safe to approach from the sides or one of us might fall in too. We don't know if the ground near there is stable. I worked on a site where there was a sinkhole," Holy smokes! "and we had to get scans of the ground and then have professionals come in to fill and secure the hole."

"So how do we get her out if we can't approach?" Angelo still looks like his heart is pounding a million miles a minute.

"Where is the hole?" I ask. "We may need to get someone to check it out."

"It's close to the lake. I told her I would get help, so she's there by herself. I didn't see anyone else nearby."

"OK, someone should go back with Angelo and post a couple signs in the area warning others so they don't fall in," I say.

"There are some orange cones around the dig site," Dr. Rossi says. "We can grab those."

"Excellent," I answer. "Could some of you do that and follow Angelo back to the hole? Place them at least ten feet away, and let Lauren know help is coming. I have an idea."

I grab Lena and Alessia and make my way back to the dig site.

"Are we going to dig her out with our trowels?" Alessia says skeptically. Come on! Shouldn't she know I have a better idea than that? Maybe I don't come off as brilliant as I think I do ...

"Definitely not." I lead them over to the cracked wall, pull out my phone, and flip on the flashlight. "Dr. Rossi let me look in here the other day. He said there is a cave behind this panel. He also said that, when he got the Lidar reading back, it showed a small hollow by the lake. What if they connect?"

"So you think Lauren could have fallen into the hollow by the lake?" Lena says.

"It's possible."

"Hang on." Lena jogs back to the tent where all the equipment and relics are housed. She returns with a huge white roll of paper. "Tore and I were looking at this earlier."

"How romantic," I say.

She sticks her tongue out at me. "It looks like there is a main tunnel and then a few side shoots. Let's bring this with us."

"Oh, we're going back through there?" Alessia suddenly looks nervous. "How do we know nothing else caved in?"

"There's no way of knowing till we start," I say, "unless you want to follow above ground and look for any cracks or collapsed ground."

"Let me see your map." Alessia pulls out her phone and takes a picture. "I'll follow above ground. At least someone will know you two went into the caves, and I can let the group by the beach know what's going on when I get there."

"Good plan," I say. "First we need to figure out how we can get back there." I jokingly push on the wall with the crack and feel it give. "You've got to be kidding me ..." I give it another little shove, and we check out the edges. There is a clear break at the bottom. It's not actually connected to the floor. When I wiggle it, it slides a bit to the right. It appears to be on casters in a groove. And I'm shocked that they are still working. "A hidden passageway maybe?"

Lena and Alessia give me a hand by digging around the bottom and far end of the wall and then shoving with me. Soon, there is a ten-inch gap, just wide enough for us to slip through into the darkness of the caves. We all hug, Lena and I flip on our lights, and we head off.

Knowing that Lauren is safe in whatever hole she fell into eases my mind a bit. Angelo said she isn't hurt, AND there is a crowd of people by the lake letting her know that help is on its way. But I'm still a little nervous. Why did I decide that I should be the one in charge? Surely someone else has been around a sinkhole before ...

Lena and I get to the first fork and unfurl the "map." We go right. Then a left. Then a long stretch of nothing. We're only in there about 20 minutes, but it seems like forever. It's much slower going than if we walk to the lake above ground because, well, it's dark. It's surprisingly not blocked anywhere that we are walking, but a couple of the side passages look like some of the earth has collapsed.

We keep going, left and right and straight when I do the inevitable and trip over a rock. I land with a thud on my left knee and hands, dropping my cell phone. "Oof."

"You OK?" Lena helps me up.

"Yeah, I'll probably have a bruise tomorrow, but I'm good." I look around for a light. "Now where is my phone?" It must have landed with the light down.

Lena walks slowly around the area where I fell, sweeping her cell phone light gently back and forth till finally—"Here ya go!" It is, indeed, face up with the light down.

I grab it, and we look at the paper again. "Please tell me you remember which fork we just passed."

Lena laughs. It carries down the passageway in a weird, haunting mocking of our situation. "I do."

She pulls a pen out of her purse and draws a few faint lines along the path we took. "We just passed this one. We go right one last time up there." She shines her flashlight ahead, and the glow is swallowed in the darkness.

"Let's do this." I mutter. Why do I feel like I'm in some army training or ghost movie or some other weird thing? This is literally a tunnel that, I have a hunch, leads to the beach.

Or maybe there are dead things in here that will suddenly reanimate and come after us. Gotta consider that too. Just in case. Because I like to be prepared. Because you can totally prepare for something like that right?

Just then, I feel a shiver under my feet. Shit.

"Another earthquake?" Lena says.

Luckily, it's a teeny one ... and hopefully the last. "We probably shouldn't be underground, should we?"

"Not the best idea, no."

"Let's keep moving then."

We get to the final fork and head to the left, as is indicated on the printout. Ahead, I see debris on the tunnel floor. Large chunks of rock piled up with leaves, branches, and maybe sand. It looks like a fine coating of dust though.

"Let's look at the Lidar," I say. Is that what you call the test results? No idea. It works. Lena knows what I'm talking about.

"This appears to connect with the hollow near the lake." Lena gestures to where we think Lauren is. "I think you're right." She points back at the debris. "Definitely looks like a cave in."

I place a foot on the pile and test it before I step up. It's a little shaky. Lena and I lock arms for stability and climb up and over the biggest pile. We skirt much of the rest of the debris easily for a few feet and then run into a bigger pile, but ...

I can see the twilight sky above. This is it!

"Lauren!" I call.

"I'm here!" Her voice ripples back out of the darkness. "Where are you?"

"In the tunnel," I say. "Close."

"There's a tunnel? Why the hell am I sitting here?"

Hmmm. She can't see the tunnel? "What can you see?"

"Not much. I dropped my phone when I fell, and it's not light enough to find it."

Just then, Lena and I round a corner and see another pile of rubble.

"I see your light!" Lauren calls. "And you're behind a huge pile of rocks."

"Lovely," I say. Lena and I eye up the pile. "Think we can move this?"

"Probably. Lauren, stay away from the rocks in case they slide."

"Will do. I'm as far away as I can be."

With one hand each, Lena and I start shifting the rocks. I move some near the bottom of the pile so some of the top ones will slide, which I find horribly clever till I realize that they will just slide wherever, and I have to watch out for them moving. Lena doesn't criticize my method, though she does have to jump out of the way a couple times for the sliding rock pile. Sorry.

After a few minutes, it seems that the pile has shifted enough that we can climb over it ... carefully. It's hip height, so I step on a few rocks and hoist my butt onto the top of the pile. Some of the rocks slide, but it works. Lena follows suit, and soon, we are both sliding down the other side into a big room.

No really, it's a room. I shine my light around and see Lauren, as well as books, a chair, a dressing table, and a few other things. On the table is a bracelet and a small bottle. Perfume maybe? "I don't think this is a cave. Someone has been here."

"This is amazing. It's been closed off from the air for so long that everything is pretty much intact." Lena paces around the room touching things that she probably shouldn't be touching.

"Are you OK to walk back with us?" I ask Lauren. No doubt she has to pee. It's been a while since she fell down here.

"Yeah, I can do that." She stands up and brushes off her pants. Little clouds of dust flitter through the air.

"Oh!" Lena cries.

"You OK?" I automatically yell.

"Yes! Oh yes! I'm soooo OK!" She sounds like something happened, and I don't get it.

"What—what is it?" I ask.

"I finally found you, *mia creatura bella*!" Lena is swooning, and I'm a little nervous of what she's talking to.

Lauren and I both approach slowly, and Lena turns, stepping aside. There, in the dark corner of the room, is a skeleton with leather cords and metal rods holding the pieces in place.

"Good grief, what is that?" I say. And then it dawns on me. "Oh," I whisper.

"This is a griffin. I knew you were here somewhere," Lena says adoringly.

"Everyone OK down there?" someone calls from above.

"We are good. Heading back to the villa with Lauren now."

"Hi girls!" It's Alessia. "I'll see you back there!"

"We called the emergency services," Angelo says, "and they are unable to make it up the road to the villa. The earthquake knocked over some dead trees. Glad you could get her that way." He sounds relieved.

As we walk down the tunnel in the opposite direction—actually, Lena is practically dancing. This has been a great day for her!—I can't help but think about how much this trip has changed me. I took charge of this rescue! That's crazy. And I went off in tunnels underground in search of my best friend. I guess when you have a big enough reason to do something, anything is possible.

"Did you talk to Angelo before you fell?" I ask Lauren.

"I did." I can hear her grinning as she talks. "He wanted to tell me that he's moving to the United States."

"Thaaat's a little soon."

"No, he's not moving for me. He is a chemist, and he interviewed with a drug company a couple months ago. They have been working on his paperwork and visa, but all the approvals finally came through."

"Oh, good for him! Is he excited about it?"

"He is. Particularly when he found out that the headquarters is near Pittsburgh."

"You're kidding!"

"He said that he knew it was in Pennsylvania and didn't realize till a couple nights ago how close it was. It's in Southpointe."

"Huh! Well, that's ... convenient." I laugh.

"Everything just works out for me." Lauren laughs too. "I guess we will be able to see each other after all."

"Is that what you want?"

"It is. I enjoy being around him. And I haven't had a relationship in a long time. I'd like to at least consider one."

I get quiet again. A relationship would definitely be nice. Maybe I had to heal from the whole Thomas incident first ... though the Big Dump was definitely a good start. Who doesn't like to kick off some major healing by making the guy who damaged you look like an ass? Or maybe it *wasn't* a good start because it sprung from two people who weren't healed from what happened to them. It *was* a little revenge-y.

Maybe I needed to run away, just for a bit, so I could grow and change outside of my comfort zone. And show myself that running away doesn't solve anything. It just allows the space for healing.

Even though I was far away from home, I didn't escape my problems. They followed me here. But I think the setting gave me the time and space to realize what I'm capable of. I thought I was taking a break, running away, but the work I ended up doing wasn't all digging in the dirt. It was internal.

For all that I had already done to create the structure of my life, I had neglected the supports. I was crumbling.

Lena's right. There is nothing more real than dirt. But you need roots to create strength. And I'm about to start planting roots. I don't feel like I need to fly anymore. It's safe to be grounded. And it will be good to be home.

Chapter 14

Home feels bizarre. First of all, it's much colder here. Like 35 degrees. No snow but definitely a festive brown and gray, as Logan said.

It's late when I walk into my house on the 21st. The air feels heavy with the promise of snow. But it probably won't. We don't get much snow before Christmas. A white one is rare.

Our friend Macy helps us get our suitcases and bags inside, and then we join Lauren in her half for a cup of tea and a short chat. Both of us are wiped, and Macy gets it.

Plus, we all work in the morning. Sort of. Lauren is her own boss, obviously, so she can basically set her own schedule. She said she has two meetings with prospective brides for summer, so I'm hoping they go well and she's not all jetlagged.

As I return to my half later, I walk in and feel the panic of all my fears, issues, and insecurities returning. Ah, my old friends. They swarm me, wrapping me in their uncomfortable yet familiar warmth, dragging me to their depths.

How the hell are you going to pull off Christmas here? It's so bitty! And the menu is all over the place. And no one will like anything you cook! You can't cook! Well, you can, but it's not like Michelin star quality, so why bother? Maybe you can pick up something from the grocery store and heat it up.

How the hell are you going to design a designer's headquarters? (My doubts have a similar pattern, which is comforting.) You don't know the first thing about that! You've only designed shops and homes and a nursing home and that one church with the sinkhole (Pits of Hell!), so this isn't going to work—

"Stop!" I actually spit this out loud and throw my scarf on the bench by the door. I can't do this anymore. I toe off my shoes, hang my coat, and flop on the couch.

What the hell was this trip even for anyway? Am I going to keep doubting myself after I flew halfway around the world and dug another century out of the ground? That's freakin' badass!

I'm badass!

I feel like a million points of light from that realization. "I'm badass," I whisper, and a chill goes down my spine. Then I realize that the thermostat is still set at 65, so I hop up and crank it up to 72.

Exhausted, even though it's only 8:30 p.m., I head up for a shower. I can take tomorrow evening to do laundry, start cleaning, and wrap presents. Planning is my forte, and I've been planning the whole month. I can do this!

It's my time to shine, bitches. I fall asleep as soon as my head hits the pillow.

———

The next morning, by the time I'm in my car, I have voice-noted myself to death.

Again, my time to shine, and I shine with lists and checking them off.

Who doesn't love a dopamine hit from checking off lists?

I take care of my first item in the car as I drive to work. I call Sal's to set up a delivery time for the mountain of toys that Declan has shipped my way. 7 p.m. tonight. Perfect.

I hang up as I'm walking into Baker & Willow, and Rachel greets me with a broad smile and a new cut and color. "Love the new 'do,' Rach. What do you call the highlight color? Wild cherry?"

"Actually, it's just 'cherry,' but I like the 'wild' bit." She laughs and hands me a couple letters that arrived while I was gone. Small envelopes. Hmmmm.

"It looks really good on you!"

"Thank you! You're such a dear. Glad you're back! Coffee's on, by the way."

I hop over to her desk and give her a huge hug. "Thank you!" Then I give her a genuine smile and just hold it for a minute. She pats me on the shoulder, and I traipse down the hall.

I feel a little different coming in here today. Almost a month off definitely lights a fire in you for getting back to work. Um, hello, I feel super refreshed. But seriously, I feel different about what I'm doing. I feel like I can be in control. I think. I might have a wobble here, but yes, more than likely, I'm in control, and I can do big things.

After I grab a coffee, yes in my PERFCT mug, I head to my desk.

Next on the to-do list ... maybe it's a ta-da list. If I can accomplish all this, I want to yell "ta-da!" Anyway, next up is the feast that I've promised my family. The list was approved. I don't have to cook everything. Sarah is bringing the dish she wanted to bring. I decided on ham ... and shrimp. Because shrimp are delightful, and I can give the dinner a little personality. Mom is making her famous sweet potatoes and her buttery dinner rolls at Grandma Claudia's before they come. So, I'm on the hook for salad, veggie trays, meats, deviled eggs (by request from Declan), and desserts.

I get on the Buggy Buddy app and order salad fixings, a ham, a bag of shrimp, two dozen eggs, mayo, some other deviled egg stuff from the recipe Declan gave me, and two pre-made veggie trays (hell yeah!).

I remember a funny meme I saw once about deviled eggs, and I chuckle. Something about the devil whispering in my ear and I whisper back that I like his eggs. Ha!

That would be really strange out of context.

Still smiling, I check my email for the confirmation from The Church Ladies.

"Having a good first day back?" Logan is leaning in my doorway, a broad grin on his face. He clearly saw me laughing about the meme. He's very holly jolly today with a green tie covered in strands of Christmas lights. Plus, the mischievous twinkle in his eyes. I realize they are a marvelous lapis color.

"I was thinking of something funny, but yes, it's good so far. Checking off my list. I have a lot going on. I was trying to take care of a few quick things before I dive into my workload. Loaded up the Buggy Buddy." Oh. My. God. Kenzi. Shut. Up.

Logan laughs, steps inside, and sits in the guest chair. "Oh good. I thought you were looking at the picture of the gingerbread house I did with my niece and nephew over the weekend. I emailed it to you. It is definitely not architect approved."

"Wouldn't pass inspection?"

"The roof fell in when I added the chimney."

"Yikes. I guess the agent would spin it as a fixer upper then."

"One can only hope."

"Were there pinwheel mints anywhere on the house?"

"Yes, two that when I picked up dinner for everyone at Two Wongs and a Wright."

"They give out mints instead of fortune cookies?"

"They have both. And I brought them specifically for the gingerbread house."

"As long as they didn't fall off, you should be fine when the house hits the market."

"Amelia snapped off part of the wall too. Still think I'll be fine? She did split it with her brother, but she showed no remorse when I said she ruined our chances of turning a profit."

I snort-laugh, and immediately clap my hand over my mouth. I know my face is turning red because I can feel the heat rising through my cheeks.

"Did you just snort?" Logan let's out a loud laugh that absolutely delights me, and I suddenly feel more at ease.

"Why yes. I did." I chuckle with him for a moment when another head pokes in the door. It's Ross, one of the marketing managers.

"Logan, we're starting in five."

"Be right there." Logan smiles at me, his bright blue eyes dancing. "I'd love to hear more about your trip. I only got little bits in your emails. I'll try to stop by later."

"Sounds good." I nod as he skips out the door to catch up with Ross. I can feel myself still grinning as I return to the confirmation email from Buggy Buddy. Pickup is tomorrow evening. That means I still have time to finish cleaning tonight, make deviled eggs on the 24th, and double-check my list.

Oh, wine! I should grab that on the way home tonight. Six adults, so four bottles should be fine. Two white, two red. Perfect!

I'm on a roll! I was born for this! I'm so organized and on top of things!

I'm proud of me.

The rest of the day is pretty smooth. I go through the mountain of email, which isn't quite as bad as it would have been because I was sneaking a login every couple days and deleting stuff I didn't need. Still though, there are a lot of emails.

My heart barrels its way into my throat when I see the one from eloise@divyashanti.com. She's scheduling a meeting with me and *my team* for January 5th at 1 p.m. Miranda is cc'd, but she hasn't responded because I'm the lead ... and I'm debating about hyperventilating.

I'm actually bouncing my legs right now as I'm thinking about how to handle this.

Wait. How would new Kenzi handle this?

She would contact Rachel and have her schedule a conference room. I pick up the phone. "Hi Rachel, it's Kenzi." Duh. She has caller ID, and I'm internal. "What conference room is available for 1 p.m. on January 5th?" I pause while she checks. "Does

Rosewater seat twenty?" I pause again. "Perfect. That should be plenty. Could you reserve that for me and *my team*?" My voice becomes pinched as I say "my team," but I manage to get it out. "Great! Thanks!"

I can do this. I email eloise@divyashanti.com back and let her know that the Rosewater conference room is reserved for us and blah blah other details that they need and some nice things that sound business-y and send!

Ha! I really did it! Now, if I don't die in the middle of that meeting, I'll really be on my way!

My phone vibrates. Mom. Checking if I ... need any help. Oh. Wow! She's just checking. Like she believes I can handle this. And I'm sure it's killing her not to ask a million questions. I bet Stan is right there holding her hand and telling her that she can do brave things!

Me: Hey Mom! I'm good. You're still bringing sweet potatoes and rolls, right?

Doesn't hurt to just confirm.

Mom: Yes! Need me to pick anything up?

Hmmmm. Maybe I should let her get the wine, since she's asking.

Me: Sure! Want to grab wine? 2 whites, 2 reds?

Mom: I can do that. And I'll get an extra rosé in case someone prefers that.

Of course she would say that.

Me: Sounds great! Thank you!

Well, it's progress. And I'm delegating. Like a grown up. I could cry I'm so proud of myself.

———

Presents were delivered on the evening of the 22nd. Along with the party food from Buggy Buddy. God, I love Buggy Buddy. Check.

Work happened on the 23rd, but nothing really exciting. Oh, but Eloise confirmed for the 5th in the Rosewater room, so um yay! If I bit my nails, though, I would totally be biting my nails. Check.

Breathe Kenzi.

Check?

I started cleaning and did laundry that night, so I'm caught up. The house is fully decorated after I added a few finishing touches. Check.

So now, it's the morning of the 24th, and I'm off from work, making deviled eggs in my pjs. Well, in my kitchen. I'm wearing pjs. It would be awkward if the eggs were in here with me, all cozy in the flannel bottoms.

I have the slightest niggle in my belly that I forgot something, but I'm a little distracted with the egg-making and the tunes.

I'm listening to Christmas music from the early 2000s on a CD that I've had forever. It has Destiny's Child on it, and the song is so awful, which makes me laugh. Normally, I loved their music, but this particular Christmas song is hilariously bad.

I guess even Beyoncé came from humble beginnings.

I'm a little disappointed that Logan never came back to my office on the 22nd or on the 23rd, since he specifically said he wanted to hear more about my trip, but I'm not going to let that bother me. I have a lot on my plate. Wooops! Including some gloppy deviled egg goo that I just splashed out of the bowl I am mixing in. I wipe it with my finger and put it back in the bowl. Don't tell. I'm clean.

But now that my list has been pretty much successfully checked off, aside from finishing the deviled eggs and actually cooking the ham, which must happen tomorrow, I feel accomplished. Not even frantic, like I thought I would.

Actually, not at all like I felt when Mom first asked me to host Christmas.

Definite progress.

My phone buzzes on the counter nearby, and I see an email notification slip over the top of the recipe I'm working on. Probably a last-minute Christmas sale email. But my gut says I should check it, so I tap on it with a clean knuckle and head over to the email app.

It's from Ottavia Zangari. Subject: Contract

Contract for what? Did I do something wrong while I was in Italy? Did I jaywalk? *Did I sign a contract before I went?*

Ultimately, I can just click on the email.

> Dearest Kenzi,
>
> It was delightful having you with us this month. I hope you enjoyed your time in our home as much as we enjoyed hosting you!

Awwwwww ...

Gianmarco and I had spoken with you about updating the blueprints for the event center so they better reflect green practices and work with the ruins that are now on our grounds. Please see the attached contract for this work, which outlines expectations, as well as the fee we are offering for your talents. If you would like to negotiate terms, please let us know soon. We would love to start working with you after the holiday.

Buone Feste,

Ottavia

To say I'm surprised will not even come close to expressing what's going on in my head right now ... and the fee that they suggest in the contract is nothing to sneeze at. It would make a hell of a dent in my house payment, be a great investment in my stock portfolio, or get me back to Italy a couple times easily.

I'll have to check that this doesn't conflict with anything I've signed at Baker & Willow before I respond, but I'm pretty sure I'm good. AND it will be a helluva way to kick off my own company ... when I'm ready. But I can at least build a portfolio. Wow!

Once the deviled eggs are done and chilling in the fridge, I do some final cleaning, grab a bite for lunch, and shower. I'm supposed to meet Lauren and Macy for dinner in Lauren's half, followed by a mini-Christmas celebration that includes wine and presents, at 6 p.m. After lounging in my bathrobe all afternoon and reading the newest Scarlet Marquez romance, I throw on a sparkly black sweater and faux leather leggings—they are plastic, so, vegan leather?—and curl my hair.

Macy's car is already in the driveway when I knock on Lauren's door at 6.

It turns out that Macy's bank closed at noon, so she and Lauren have been wrapping presents together for a couple hours. I was oblivious because my nose was in the book I mentioned. SUCH a good book! I was right at the part where Ayla and Jake—

"Kenz?"

"Sorry. What's that?"

"Can I get you a glass of cranberry Riesling?" Macy has a bottle hovering over a glass because, clearly, I'm going to say "yes."

"Yes please."

"Chinese should be here soon," Lauren adds. "We can do presents while we wait." She adds a little shoulder shimmy, scoops up her glass of

Riesling, and struts to the tree. "I'm excited." Clearly.

She pushes aside a couple big boxes for her niece, Sage, and digs out two packages that look like they have store-bought sweaters in them, just judging from the box shape and size.

But it's *Lauren*, so I know they aren't store-bought sweaters, and my heart skips a beat because this is going to be so good.

Macy has shredded the wrapping on hers, her coffee-colored corkscrew curls bouncing furiously as she does so. "Oh! This is perfect!" Macy is the queen of maxi dresses with her long limbs and slim frame, so the dress Lauren has created for her is bound to be stunning on her. It's a geometric print in emerald, white, and navy. She jumps up and holds the dress in front of her, "modeling" it. It's sleeveless, so she should be able to throw on a sweater or suit jacket for work and wear it out for dinner or drinks in the evening.

I admire Macy's dress and the way it makes her ebony skin glow for a moment before opening my package. There is a lot of red. Old Kenzi would have been a little nervous to have on that much red ... it's like a stoplight in the middle of the room. New Kenzi is ... well, adjusting to the idea.

I pull the dress out of the box and stand too. It's a serious blue-red. Flowy, flouncy, and very feminine. Knee-length, wrap style top, billowy sleeves. It's a statement for sure. And with my dark hair and pale—let's say "porcelain" and make me sound fancy—skin, it's bound to turn heads. In a good way.

"I can't believe you made this for me! Thank you!" I tear up as I think about the painstaking hours that Lauren put into our presents. Old Kenzi would have felt guilty about my purchased present, but I know that I put just as much love into what I picked for my friends as Lauren did into this dress.

As we're opening the presents from me and from Macy, the doorbell rings, and I jog over to answer it. Looking forward to some Singapore noodles!

But the man at the door is holding a big box and a tablet for me to digitally sign. "This can't possibly be lo mien," I deadpan.

"Not today. Didn't have enough fortune cookies for a box this big."

I chuckle, double-check the name—yep, it's Lauren—and sign for the box.

"Last minute presents?" I ask. Lauren frowns and shakes her head.

"Not expecting anything." She takes the box from me. "It's from Italy." Gently, she cuts the tape with scissors because the box says NOT to use a knife. And she extracts three smaller boxes, labeled "M," "L," and "K."

"Medium, large, and ... kid-sized?" I say. Probably not, but it made me laugh.

"Macy, Lauren, and Kenzi, goofball," Lauren says. She hands a box to each of us, and we open them.

Finally! I can't believe that I am standing here holding a pair of gorgeous raspberry suede Zangari loafers in my hands, and they are actually *mine*! I slip them on and prance, yes prance, because that's what you do in these fabulous shoes. So comfortable! I may never take them off again. When I finally decide to descend from the clouds, I see that Lauren has a pair of pumpkin-colored loafers and Macy's are sky blue. All lovely!

And now we are *all* prancing.

A note from Gianmarco in the box clarifies who the loafers are for. Why did he send some for Macy? He expressed that since Macy was unable to join us on the trip due to her own vacation, he wanted her to have a pair. And he wants all of us to visit soon!

Cori Wamsley

The doorbell rings again, and it's finally the Chinese food, so we dig in. Two Wongs and a Wright make the most amazing Singapore noodles, which yes, are gluten-free ... I feel like I should explain the name of the restaurant. Eric and Jamie Wong are brothers who went into business with their friend Alex Wright, and the combination of names for their restaurant couldn't have been more perfect. Yes, they are also all Chinese—Alex's mom is actually from Guangdong Province.

Their back story is on the back of the menu. I haven't actually talked to them.

Interrupting my reverie, my phone vibrates in my pocket. It's Miranda. She sent a merry Christmas text with a little tree, star, and package emojis. She's the best boss. I text back a snowman, ornament, tree, and *Merry Christmas*, and my phone buzzes again.

Miranda: I'm excited for your meeting with the Divya Shanti team! Enjoy the holidays!

I pause, but I really can share my emotions here.

Me too! Thanks! Happy holidays!

I think I'm growing up. Tear.

As we clean up, Macy refills our wine, and then we retreat back to the living room.

"Guys, it's been a year since we all became friends, and I can't imagine my life without you." Macy puts a hand over her heart and gives us the gushy closed mouth smile that means she will probably tell us how much she loves us. Thanks wine! "I just love you guys so much!"

"Mace, we've known each other longer than a year. You modeled for me before the pandemic." Lauren swirls her wine and pushes the delicious suede loafers off, pulling her legs up so she's curled on the couch.

"I know, but we only met Kenzi last fall, and I feel like our family of besties is complete now."

"It's been quite a year! And I can't imagine meeting anyone else in quite the same way!" I swig back half the glass of wine. Not sure why. I don't like "need a drink," but the creamy cranberry notes just feel soothing as they slide down my throat. It's comfort wine. "In fact, I hope I never meet anyone the same way again!"

That gets some hearty chuckles from the girls.

Lauren starts getting teary eyed. "You know, we never did celebrate the anniversary of the Big Dump! We should have done some sort of moonlight ceremony where we chant around a fire in the woods and howl at the moon."

Cori Wamsley

We all laugh. That would be perfect.

"I thought the trip to Italy was pretty appropriate," I say. "Of course, we wish you could have come too, Macy."

"I do too, but I'm glad you could both go. You deserved it after the way Thomas treated you. That was unbelievable. Trips like that tend to help you heal in a big way. So, you can, you know, move forward."

I sip the Riesling and agree. And the strangest sense of calm washes over me. I don't feel like running anymore. I feel ... at home. Good.

"Think you'll stick around a bit longer, Kenzi?" Macy asks.

"I think I want to do that *and* do some more traveling. I want to live bigger. But I also know I need roots. And honestly, I'm happy here. Especially with you guys."

Lauren cries first, and then I cry, and then Macy is just laughing but switches to crying because, for some reason, Lauren and I are the Typhoid Marys of becoming a weepy mess.

"I don't know how I would have made it through the last year without you guys, and now that I feel all grounded and safe here again, I can't imagine going elsewhere and trying to find this again. I love it here, and maybe this is where I belong." I have to dash to the bathroom for a tissue at this point because my nose suddenly does that you're-crying-so-let's-randomly-get-really-runny thing. How does that make sense evolutionarily? Who is crying and needs their nose to run? *Oh no, I'm super emotional! Let's get snot involved!*

I digress.

Then Lauren starts babbling. "I know that we are all strong independent women, but I feel like I'm finally ready to have a relationship too, you know, and with Angelo moving here, maybe something will finally work."

"I hope it does!" I say. I'm thrilled for her. Not upset. Not jealous. Not nervous about him turning out to be a jerk. Really just happy.

And that's good. I feel good. It's about time.

After innumerable (which I can't even pronounce I my head because I think I had a whole bottle of wine by myself) hugs, I return to my half of the duplex for bed.

My phone lights up as I enter the front hall. It's Mom.

Merry Christmas, love! See you tomorrow!

Cori Wamsley

Merry Christmas, Mom!

Chapter 15

After all I've been through in the past month, now I'm about to pull off Christmas lunch! I am pretty damn proud!

I am wearing my brand new custom-made crimson dress by Lauren Hunter, the designer, my bestie. And I feel pretty amazing. Normally I would have felt weird in such a bold color, but I checked myself out in the mirror—nice legs, Kenz!—so I'm feeling pretty confident. Maybe I'll wear this outside of my house someday and around people I'm not related to.

I prep the veggie trays ... by removing the lids. This was such a good move. I pull out the cookies from The Church Ladies. So cute! They are a variety: cutouts with sweet-smelling icing, gingerbreads with adorable cinnamon buttons and little details in white icing, chocolate chip, sugar cookies, gluten-free peanut butter cookies in a separate container (yay!), and Rice Krispie treats. There is a tray of nuts, olives, and crackers that Lauren accidentally got two of and gave me one. (Thanks to the guy who messed up her Buggy Buddy order just this little bit!) When Declan's gunmetal gray Suburban pulls into the drive, I pop the deviled eggs out to join the rest of the snacks.

The girls tumble out of the car in matching candy cane dresses and green leggings. The boys are in dress pants and probably sweaters. I can't see past their coats. I glance back at the tree, which is proudly hovering over an absolute mountain of presents between stuff from the guy in red and me. Santa and I make a good team!

Declan and Sarah hop out of the car too, but you know, they are basically security detail when they are rolling with their kids, who I can't wait to squeeze! And spoil. I'm the best auntie.

The ham smells good in the oven, not smelling burnt at all, so I'm happy about that. Mom's sweet potatoes smell amazing, and the rolls do too—but I can't eat those, so I'm team sweet potato all the way.

We have some time before the ham is ready, so obviously, Huxley, my oldest nephew, suggests that we open presents. Smart man at age 12!

I wrap my arm around the closest kiddo, Lennox, and guide her to the tree. The rest rampage through my house to the tree and start tearing into their stuff. So. Much. Stuff.

I'm pretty proud of the presents I got them. Lennox did indeed like the flamingo roller skates. And wrist guards. And helmet. If I could bubble wrap those kiddos, I would. Probably a bad idea though.

"Good call on the wrist guards, Kenzi," Mom says. I'm actually proud of my ability to predict disaster, so this is a nice compliment.

Hux wanted a new game for his whatever system, so that was pretty easy. Especially since Declan sent me a link when I couldn't figure it out. I got him some game currency to spend on gear in the game too, so I'm totally in the favorite aunt zone now.

Reese is very happy with new clothes for her doll and a pretty princess dress for her that matches one of the doll dresses. Six is the best age. I could be six right now and be perfectly happy with the same things. Heck, I would probably be delighted with them even today.

"Oh, Reesey, you can match Lorelai now!" Sarah exclaims.

"Lorelai loves matching her mommy," Reese replies as she does a little dance with the new dress in front of her. Girl, I know that feeling!

Griff wants to write and draw graphic novels, so he got a set of special pencils, an art pad, and a couple drawing books. One of them is for graphic novels, but the other ... totally my pick, hoping he likes it. It's a how-to-draw-houses book. I know. An architect trying to get her nephew to draw houses. Maybe we can do it together. Ya never know!

The oven buzzes, and I pull the ham out. It still smells good and definitely didn't burn, so yay! I set it on the stove and pass the electric knife to Stan because he's the meat handler in our family. He starts slicing off chunks as Reese and Lennox cover their ears and run to the corner. It's pretty loud. Even with ten people talking, which was already loud.

Grandma Claudia envelops me in a big hug. "Kenzi, this looks wonderful. What a great job!"

"Thanks Grandma!" I'm touched that she's so impressed, and for a second, I think, "Did she think I couldn't do it?" but then I switch back to just gratitude because she probably never doubted me at all. Jennifer Halliday says not to put your crappy ideas about yourself in other people's heads, so I'm taking this as a win.

Mom puts a hand on my shoulder, "Really Kenzi, this looks so good. That ham smells heavenly. This is perfect." She then puts both her hands on my shoulders and looks me squarely in the eye. "I'm sure all my poking and prodding was a nuisance, but I just wanted to help. I'm sorry if I pushed a little too hard."

I really don't know what to say. She realized that she was pushing me over the edge. "Mom, thanks. I'm glad you felt like you could trust me to do this. I know you just wanted to help." I give her a hug. "And it was pretty fun."

"I'm glad you liked doing this. I remember the first time I had a big family meal—"

"Oh no!" Sarah is holding a big spoon over the pot of bamia—Lebanese okra stew—that she brought with her. "I forgot to turn the stove on to warm this up. Can we delay like 20 minutes?"

"Yeah, not a problem." I quickly point at the right knob for her, and she jacks it to medium heat. Mom is engrossed in a chat with Declan now, so I wander into the living room to check out the chaos.

"I love my presents Mercedes-Kenz."

"I love you Gryffindor." My nephew and I have been coming up with clever nicknames for each other for a couple years now, which is pretty hard considering our names aren't common or part of other words. Often, we are Mercedes-Kenz and Gryffindor. Which is cute. It's our thing.

He holds up the first page in his new art pad. "I'm drawing a house for you to live in when you have kids."

"Oh my God, you are?" I take the notebook and stare at the lovely home he's designing for me. It has a porch that looks a lot like the one on the how-to-draw-a-porch page of the book he's holding. "I'm impressed." And really struggling not to cry. How sweet is this?

And then I have the strangest realization. This is what I was looking for. Belonging. Love. Home. It was here—well in Paris since that's where Declan had the family the past few months, but you know, in my world—all along.

"Let's take a picture together." I wrap an arm around him. "Hold up your drawing." The notebook is in front of us, open to the page with the house. I set the timer on my phone, stretch my arm as far as I can, and we both grin at the camera. Me and my little buddy. "You're quite an artist, you know?"

"I'm going to be a famous graphic novelist someday." He grins and then drops his voice to a whisper. "But I like drawing houses too."

"Dude, you can do both. You don't have to choose one thing, and certainly not right now!" I tip my head thoughtfully. "Do you mind if I send this picture to my friend? I think she would like to see it."

"No, that's fine." He returns to drawing, and I pull up a text to Lena, attaching the picture.

Hey! *Buon Natale*! (Merry Christmas) I wanted to send you a picture of me with my favorite Griffin.

That's my nephew's name. Looks like we both found griffins!

A few moments later, a text comes through from her.

Buon Natale! What a sweet picture! He is certainly a treasure! So glad you have him! Enjoy the day with your family!

As I'm grinning at her text, a picture comes through from her end. Lena and Tore, each holding a glass of wine, his arm around her. And they look over the moon.

Wow. I'm so happy for them!

I head to the kitchen for one more check of the food. I don't want to get halfway through the meal and realize we didn't get Sarah's muhammara— Lebanese red pepper and walnut dip—out of the fridge.

It all looks good. All the food is out. Just waiting on Sarah to give the approval for her stew. "A few more minutes. Still not warm enough," she says.

So, I pour a glass of wine. Mom picked my favorite white, a pear Chablis by Lavender Fields Vineyards, which is local. It tastes especially good knowing that I pulled off something I thought a month ago was impossible.

As I sip and glance around at the festivities, I really couldn't be more proud. And then, my heart stops beating altogether. I forgot to get a special dessert for Grandma Claudia! It's the only thing she requested. But she doesn't really do tech, so I didn't copy her on the spreadsheet I sent out to make sure we had everything on the list for today. Ugh!

I feel absolutely horrible. I'm the worst granddaughter! And she didn't even say anything about it. It was supposed to be perfect. It almost was. And then I screwed it up. She must think—

Now I'm spiraling. I feel really guilty. Are there levels of guilty? I'm at like Olympic level. And it's Christmas day. NOTHING is open. I can't just run out and get something. I wonder if I have a bottle of spice wine that I can give her to dip the gingerbread cookies in.

This is a nightmare.

No. This is fine.

Well, not really. I still feel guilty. I have to push this down. I take a deep breath and count to four as I breath out. Then I do square breathing, which I read about in the superpowers book. In four, hold four, out four, hold four. I can still feel my heart throbbing in my throat. I do the breathing exercise again and again.

Crap.

Grandma ... I'm sorry? Ugh.

As I'm taking another sip of wine and planning how to fix this, the doorbell rings.

My house grows oddly quiet as we all look at each other. Everyone is here, and I'm not expecting anything or anyone. I mean, it's Christmas day, so who is going to deliver today?

Pulling myself together, I set the wine down, smooth my dress, and head for the door. A peek through the window beside the door shows me that it's Logan. *What?*

Self-conscious now, since I'm wearing the flaming red dress and just had a near heart attack, I straighten my necklace and open the door. I realize that I'm just staring at him, smoothing the ruffles of my dress, twisting my blue beaded bracelet, and haven't said a word.

"Hi!" he says from the other side of the door. He looks nice. Well, he always looks nice. But he's wearing his work coat, a lovely gray wool that makes his eyes look the color of steel reflecting the sky. I finally notice that he's holding a round container. Huh.

"Sorry, I wasn't expecting anyone else," I say. I open the storm door and motion for him to come in. "Merry Christmas!"

"Thanks, merry Christmas!" Logan replies. He steps into the warm entry of my home and eyes up the pile of guest shoes beside my shoe bench. Mine are all neatly tucked into the bench, so obviously, my guests had to leave theirs literally everywhere.

Also, it's oddly silent for the number of people here. I peer around and realize that everyone is listening or peeking at us around the support beam in the living room.

After a moment, Logan and I are looking at each other in silence. "Soooo," I begin. "What's up?"

For once, Logan actually doesn't seem as calm and confident as he always does at the office. He stumbles through something about being "on my way out" and "thought I'd pop over" and "wanted to bring you this."

"Oh? Thank you!" I say. My eyebrow is cocked perplexedly as I smile. He brought me a present? "What is *this*?" I say as he thrusts the box into my arms. I take a couple steps toward the kitchen and set it on the counter. Now, unfortunately, everyone can see me, and my cheeks are rapidly changing color to match my dress.

"It's a, uh, boozy gluten-free plum pudding," he says, still sounding a little bashful. "I wanted to check all the boxes, so it's safe for you and had the kick your grandma wanted. You mentioned that she wanted to have a boozy dessert, and I love to bake. I know you were really busy after you returned from your trip. I thought I might help out and surprise you." He clears his throat. "I made sure everything was clean: ingredients, counter, bowls ... so it's definitely gluten-free."

I am possessed by the inundating force of relief coursing through my body and immediately throw my arms around him in a giant hug. I hear Mom, Grandma, and Sarah all saying "aw" in the background, but I am actually not embarrassed. I'm owning this. What a sweet thing to do! "You're amazing. Thank you!" I squeeze, and he finally wraps his arms around me too. "You just saved me. Right before you showed up, I realized I forgot dessert."

Logan laughs as we both let go, and he meets my adoring gaze. "It's a lot for one person. I thought you might need it."

"Seriously thank you!"

"Yes, thank you!" Grandma Claudia says. Chuckles echo through the room.

I pop the lid off. It smells like brandy and is decorated with little chunks of dried fruit. "You're really talented. Does this taste as good as it looks?"

Logan grins. "I made one a few days ago to practice. I took it to my sister's over the weekend for the present wrapping party, and it was gone in an hour. I hope you guys like it." He turns to walk toward the door, but I put my hand on his arm.

"Are you going to see your family?"

"I thought I would stop by early and just hang out. My brother-in-law loves football, so I'll probably grab a beer and just watch with him till everyone arrives for dinner."

"Oh, then you have time, honey." Grandma Claudia is at the door suddenly, and she slips her hand through his arm. "If you're going to bring us a cake, I'll be damned if you don't get a piece."

"I really made it for you guys. It's no bother at all." He chuckles as my grandmother somehow gets him to take off his coat and shoes and enter the kitchen.

"Nonsense. You need to enjoy the fruits of your labor," Grandma insists. She plucks a chunk of dried fruit from the top of the cake and makes a face like it's delicious. "Tastes like brandy."

"We were actually about to have lunch," I say. "Would you like to join us?" I am shocked by my own boldness.

"You already have your shoes off, so that's a 'yes.'" Grandma has a plate in her hand and is already getting a slice of pudding. She winks at me, and I just shake my head.

"It's a 'yes' then," Logan says.

"I'm glad to hear it." I point at him and laughingly call out, "Everyone, this is Logan." The response is a smattering of kids laughing loudly because they are focused on their new stuff, adults saying "hi" and waving, and me looking tenderly at someone who went out of his way to do something so kind for me. I thought he was just a work acquaintance a few weeks ago. Funny how things change ...

"The cake was really just an excuse to get fed." Logan takes the plate I offer him as we both laugh and get in line behind all the adults helping kids prepare their plates. "I had to handle a last-minute client emergency the last couple days of work, so I didn't make it back to your office. Now you can tell me all the details of your trip that I didn't get in your emails."

"I have some stories," I say. I actually thought he was blowing me off, which didn't make sense, but you know, head trash.

"I'd love to hear them." Then he looks at me soberly. "You know, for months I've wanted to talk to you. It will be nice to get to know you better."

"It will," I whisper. As he turns to grab a roll, I close my eyes for a moment, and I swear I can feel the ground quiver.

Acknowledgements

This was such a fun story to write, and I was almost sad to see the production process come to an end because it meant I didn't get to play in Kenzi's world anymore.

Kenzi, my main character, came bouncing into my world in December of 2021 with a tangled bunch of ideas that didn't really lead me anywhere until I figured out who she was, what she needed to heal, and how we could do it.

She was incredibly fun to write with her quirky cleverness and her overly self-conscious vibe. It felt like I was pulling from so many women I know who started their journeys like this and then found their confidence and themselves along the way.

I chose Italy as Kenzi's "crucible for change" because of the vibe I got when I visited Rome and Florence so many years ago on my honeymoon. I also chose it because of the ruins and the potential for finding things in the dirt that are literally thousands of years old.

Several things inspired the story. First, of course, Kenzi's character and her need to develop into the amazing woman she became. But also, I was watching a lot of documentaries about archeological digs in Europe over the summer of 2022. My husband and I love history, and we particularly enjoy watching these together. In the middle of one that took place in Italy, lightning struck. I jumped up from the couch and ran to my office.

I had recalled a book I bought almost 20 years ago that focused on two of my favorite subjects coming together: mythology and archaeology. I bought the book because of a show I watched where they interviewed a scientist, Adrienne Mayor, about her theory of where stories about mythical creatures originated. They had to come from somewhere, right?

She hypothesized that the ancients found bones that didn't look like any creatures they were familiar with and, much like with their nature or seasons myths, wanted to make sense of the world around them.

So they came up with giants and centaurs and Pegasus and all the other amazing beings that we love to hear about in those stories. What I found so amazing was that she matched up the origin of the myths with bone beds in Italy and Greece that could have supplied the impetus for these stories to people thousands of years ago, and the maps overlapped perfectly.

When I rushed to my office, I grabbed the book—*The First Fossil Hunters: Paleontology in*

Greek and Roman Times—and re-read several pieces of it. In particular, I liked the idea of including griffins in Kenzi's story because Roman emperors claimed to have their skeletons. It was a perfect fit again.

The Treasures We Seek had been slow going till that point. Then, I finally pulled together the outline for the final version of Kenzi's story and began writing with fresh fervor.

About a month later, I grabbed coffee with my friend Marta Mazzoni, who had just signed on to be part of the book *Unleashing Your Soul-Level Magic*, an anthology published by my publishing house, Aurora Corialis Publishing, featuring the stories of 12 women sharing how they overcame challenges and discovered their gifts. We talked about some of her story ideas for her chapter, and I asked her some coaching questions like, "What's a major turning point in your life? What is a moment that changed everything for you?"

She said, "Maybe the first time I flew." Then she told me how she had broken up with her college boyfriend (because he took a job several states away), searched online for something to perk her up because she was so down from the breakup, and found a listing for a call for volunteers that intrigued her. They were looking for people to come to Italy for an archeological dig, so she signed up, booked a flight, and took off on a major life-changing adventure just a few weeks later.

I felt chills when she said that. It was so similar to the outline I had written that I knew the Universe was telling us both that these are the stories we need to write.

A year later, I was almost ready to release *The Treasures We Seek*!

I'd like to thank Marta for that conformational nudge on my story, along with Adrienne Mayor for penning her ideas and inspiring a woman in her early 20s to make connections and be curious.

I'd also like to thank my beta readers for their insights. Stefania Forte, you took this book to the next level! There are so many nuances when you're crossing borders that help show that you really get the culture, and though I researched and tried to cover all of them, you certainly helped me with things I didn't even think of! The food and wine that screams Castel Gandolfo, Italy, in this book is largely in part to Stefania's eye. Thank you!

Amy Hooper Hanna, Rita Smith, and Kelli Komondor, you guys gave me so many great pointers about things that, of course, made sense in my head, but didn't for the reader. I appreciate the questions! This is why I love having beta readers who love to read. They are great about mentioning all the little things! Thank you to all of you!

Also, thank you to those who provided praise, commented about the story on social, and generally supported me during the journey from crazy idea to finished book!

A special thank you goes to Allison Hrip, my editor, who always helps my characters and my storylines shine! And to Karen Captline, my "cover girl," who has created some of the most beautiful wrappings for not only my stories, but also most of the books that we publish through Aurora Corialis Publishing. You two are truly talented gems, and I'm so glad I have you both in my life!

Finally, I want to thank my husband, Matt, and my daughters, London and Talia, for listening to me talk about my characters and the exciting things they were doing as I burst out of my office after a writing session. I know it's crazy living with a creative, but I hope it's at least fun!

And to my readers: If you've read this far, thank you. I greatly appreciate my readers and hope they enjoy learning about the journey. If you've enjoyed this book, I would love an Amazon review!

Questions for Deeper Reading

1. If your best friend suggested going on an archaeological dig, would you pack up and go?
2. When Kenzi is debating about the trip, she jokes that she's not doing another cleanse with Lauren. Do you think that her trip ended up being a "cleanse" of sorts?
3. Have you been to a foreign country? What lasting impact did that have on you?
4. Should Kenzi have approached Ella's relationship troubles a different way? Or kept her nose out altogether?
5. When the women went to Rome, Julie shared Lauren's role of sage in the story. How do you relate to Julie's message of making adventure a habit?
6. Have you ever felt the ground quiver when you've been somewhere or experienced something special?
7. Kenzi often feels embarrassed by her celiac disease. Do you have friends with conditions or illnesses? How do you show them that you care and make sure that they aren't left out because of their medical issues?
8. Did it surprise you that Kenzi calmed down when she focused more on the world around her and really soaking it in? Have you done any grounding exercises like thinking about your

five senses to help regulate your mood? Does that work for you?

9. What did the griffin represent to Lena? What is your "griffin"?

10. Would you let yourself have a holiday romance as Lauren did? Why or why not?

11. Kenzi knows when she's talking with Gianmarco about the event center that architecture is truly her jam and it brings out a creative and passionate side of her if she just lets go. What does that for you? Or are you searching for it still?

12. Who do you relate to most in *The Treasures We Seek*? Why?

About the Author

Cori Wamsley, CEO of Aurora Corialis Publishing, works with business owners who have a transformational story to share and has helped over 200 people become authors. She coaches them to easily write and publish a book for their brand that helps them create a legacy and be seen as an expert while building a relationship with the reader.

Many of the books that Cori has helped publish benefit nonprofits, including Alina's Light, KindLeigh, The Backpack Program, and Young Adult Survivors United. Cori believes that books are a gift that can give beyond words and is proud to work with authors who want to benefit others with their writing efforts.

Cori and her clients have been interviewed for a variety of podcasts, TV shows, and publications, including *Dr. Phil*; *The TODAY Show*; Tampa, Florida News 9; JET 24 (yourerie.com); *The Pittsburgh Post-Gazette*; *The New York Telegraph*; Medium; Thrive Global; and more.

Cori has 18 years' experience as a professional writer and editor, including 10 years with the Departments of Energy and Justice and four years as the executive editor of *Inspiring Lives Magazine*. She also wrote nine fiction books and one nonfiction book and contributed chapters to two anthologies. Cori has been a contributor to multiple publications, including *Brainz Magazine* and *Authority Magazine*.

Cori holds a master's and bachelor's in English literature and a bachelor's in biology from West Virginia University. She lives in Pittsburgh, Pa., with her husband and two daughters. When she's not helping others write and publish their books, she's working on her next novel.

Connect with Cori at www.auroracorialispublishing.com or on Facebook or Instagram at @CoriWamsley.

Printed in the USA
CPSIA information can be obtained
at www.ICGtesting.com
JSHW022231031123
51450JS00006B/47